Shandra Higheagle Mystery Series

Double Duplicity

Tarnished Remains

Deadly Aim

Murderous Secrets

Killer Descent

Reservation Revenge

Yuletide Slaying

Fatal Fall
A Shandra Higheagle Mystery

Paty Jager

Windtree Press
Hillsboro, OR

This is a work of fiction, Names, characters, places, and incidents either are the product of the author's imagination or are used fictitiously, and any resemblance to actual persons living or dead, business establishments, events, or locales, is entirely coincidental.

FATAL FALL

Contact Information: info@windtreepress.com

Windtree Press
Hillsboro, Oregon
http://windtreepress.com

Cover Art by Christina Keerins

Published in the United States of America

ISBN 9781944973889

This book is dedicated to a group of people who are willing to help authors make sure the legal, crime, and forensics in our books are accurate. Thank you specialists at the Crimescene yahoo loop. You, and my first responder son-in-law, are always willing to answer my questions.

Chapter One

Shandra stepped into the Huckleberry Medical Clinic as a police siren came to life. She glanced out the glass door and watched a police car speed up the street. The shrill whine faded as the vehicle turned the corner.

"Miss Higheagle, Dr. Porter isn't back from lunch. Please have a seat," the day nurse, Shyanne Dover said, glancing up from the book she was reading.

"Do you know when he'll be in?" Shandra covered a cough with a tissue. She'd started coughing last week and it wasn't going away. She had to be better in two weeks. The money she paid for a booth at the prestigious pottery show in New Mexico was non-refundable. This show was held every April. She had several repeat buyers who came to the show for her newest vase.

Shyanne glanced at the clock to the side of the reception desk. "He's fifteen minutes late. Dr. Porter is never late."

The phone rang.

"Huckleberry Medical Clinic, this is Shyanne, how may I help you?" the receptionist answered.

Her usual smile dropped from her face. "I'm sorry, Dr. Porter hasn't returned from lunch." She listened. "Yes. I understand. You can call his cell phone." Shyanne held the phone away from her face and glared at the handset. "Being the police and all, I would think you already have his cell number since he's the medical examiner."

Shandra chuckled. It wouldn't surprise her if the policeman on the other end of the phone was Officer Blane. He tended to act before he thought.

The receptionist rattled off a number and dropped the receiver onto the phone with a clatter. "That man should have never been made a policeman. He's rude."

"Does this mean I might as well reschedule my appointment to tomorrow?" Shandra asked, walking up to the desk.

"I guess. I don't really know. They said there was a problem at Gladys Narvel's place." She leaned forward. "That's Dr. Porter's aunt. The one he lives with."

"Oh. I hope it isn't anything serious." Her mind was already whirling. That had to be Blane who tore down the street not ten minutes ago. Wouldn't whoever called the police have also called Dr. Porter?

"Where does Mrs. Narvel live?" Shandra thought a quick peek at what was happening couldn't hurt anything. She'd helped solve several murders the last couple of years. While she had a knack for it, she didn't go looking for trouble.

"It's the large, Victorian house on the way to the ski lodge. Her husband was the backer for Huckleberry Ski Resort." The younger woman appeared about to burst with the need to tell her more.

"Really? I thought Sydney Doring was one of the owners." She pulled a tissue from the box sitting on the counter and covered another coughing fit.

Shyanne nodded. "He is part owner. Mrs. Narvel owns most of the resort. When her husband got tired of working so much, he sold forty percent to Mr. Doring. He was to take over the day to day running."

"I've lived here for nearly eight years and I didn't know that. Thanks." Shandra slung the strap of her purse over her shoulder and left the clinic. A quick trip past the Narvel house couldn't hurt anything. Dr. Porter was a quiet, closed off person, but she had a feeling it was more about his lack of social skills than his keeping people away. It would be interesting to learn more about him.

She climbed into her Jeep, fending off Sheba, her large, fluffy, cowardly dog. "I don't have anything for you to eat. I was at the doctor's office, not a restaurant."

A wide muzzle and wet nose sniffed her shoulder and neck.

"Cut that out." Another coughing fit had her grabbing a tissue. When she could breathe again, Shandra pulled out of the clinic parking lot. At the stop sign, waiting to turn onto Huckleberry Street, the street that would take her out of town and to the ski resort, she spotted Ryan's county SUV go by, with the light at the top of his windshield flashing and a siren screeching.

"I wonder what Ryan is investigating this direction," she said to Sheba. Being a detective with the Weippe County Sheriff's Office, he was called out on many sundry events. She smiled remembering how she'd met him. He'd been called to investigate the murder of a gallery owner. She'd found the body and was the first suspect. That murder had brought them together and now they lived together with talk of a marriage in the future.

She poked his number on her Bluetooth screen. Then had second thoughts and turned it off. He didn't mind hearing from her, however, if he was working, she wouldn't want him asking her what she was doing.

She turned the corner and followed him down the street. He picked up speed outside of town. She continued at the speed limit.

Several miles out of town, she spotted the large Victorian house she'd always wondered about when driving to the ski lodge. A police car and Ryan's SUV sat in the driveway. A single row of daffodils lined the cobblestone drive.

"I wonder if Blane was able to contact Dr. Porter?" She patted Sheba's big head when the dog poked it between the front seats. "I wonder why Blane called Ryan?"

Even knowing how much Ryan complained

about civilians getting in the way during a preliminary investigation, she couldn't stop herself from turning up the driveway. She'd never met Mrs. Narvel and she didn't know Dr. Porter all that well, but she couldn't shake the feeling she needed to know what was happening.

She exited the Jeep and walked up the pretty cobbled walkway to the porch.

The house was an impressive three-story Victorian with a conservatory on the east side and a front porch that stretched the length of the front of the house. There appeared to be a basement, making the whole structure, including the tower, five stories.

The double doors stood open and yellow crime scene tape stretched across the opening.

Ryan knelt beside a body at the bottom of the stairs.

Shandra leaned against the door jamb. From what she could see, it was an older woman. Mrs. Narvel?

A car skidded to a stop in the concrete drive. Dr. Porter swung the car door open and jogged up onto the porch.

"Did you find her?" he asked Shandra.

"No…I—"

Before she could say any more, Officer Blane stood in the doorway. "Dr. Porter, I'm afraid I'll have to take your statement outside." Blane glared at her and ducked under the crime scene tape to stand on the porch.

"I'm the medical examiner. I need to…" Dr.

Porter brushed a hand across his eyes. "I need to see my aunt."

"She's dead." Ryan's voice at her shoulder, spun Shandra to face him. Irritation narrowed his eyes, before he turned his attention to Dr. Porter. "You can't do anything for her, and because she's family, I've called in the ME from Warner."

Ryan put a hand on Shandra's arm. "Blane, don't question him until I get back." He escorted her back to her Jeep.

"What are you doing here?"

She started coughing and dug in her purse for a tissue.

Ryan handed her a clean red bandana from somewhere on his person. "I hope you aren't coughing just to get my sympathy."

Shaking her head, Shandra finished coughing, blew her nose, and pointed to the doctor. "I was at the clinic for my appointment with Dr. Porter when Blane called asking for him. Shyanne, the receptionist, told me what Blane said and where to find this house." She waved her hand. "It's a beautiful piece of architecture."

"Why did you feel the need to come here?" Ryan waved the bandana away when she attempted to return it.

"I don't know. I guess hearing the siren, the call, and knowing it was Dr. Porter's aunt…I was just compelled to come see." She had learned from their first meeting, if she told Ryan the truth, he tended to allow her more insight into the crimes than he should.

"She fell down the stairs. We won't know anything else until an autopsy is done. Go home. Drink fluids and rest." He kissed her temple. "I'll be home the usual time."

Shandra smiled, slid into the Jeep, and started it up. As she backed down the driveway, she watched Ryan walk back to Blane and Dr. Porter. At the side of the house, she noticed a young woman in yoga pants and sweatshirt peek around the corner at the men.

Chapter Two

Ryan shook his head as he walked back to Blane and Doc Porter. He should have known with Shandra in town, she'd discover an untimely death. At least she hadn't been dreaming about her grandmother and Dr. Porter. If she had, he would have never been able to get her away. While he believed in her dreams, he didn't like how they managed to get Shandra involved in dangerous situations.

Dr. Porter had the young officer pushed up against the crime scene tape in the doorway. "I don't understand why I can't see my aunt. She's the only family I had left."

He felt for the doctor, but considering the marks he'd spotted on the woman's wrists, he didn't think her fall was an accident.

"Doctor, when was the last time you spoke with

your aunt?" Ryan asked, drawing his notepad from a shirt pocket.

Dr. Porter turned his light blue eyes on Ryan. As many times as he'd worked with the man as a medical examiner, this was the first time he'd witnessed any emotion in his icy gaze. He appeared truly devastated. His pale complexion added to his look of distress.

"I left for the clinic at my usual time of seven-thirty. Gladys and Jeffery were in the dining room."

"Jeffery who? What was he doing in the dining room with your aunt?" Ryan wondered how many people lived in the massive house.

"Jeffery Holmes, he's, was, writing my aunt's memoirs. She commissioned him about six months ago. He's been living in the house." The doctor ran a hand through his short-cropped white hair. "My aunt has COPD, a breathing ailment. She has to use oxygen all day." His cool gaze peered at Ryan. "She didn't trip over her oxygen tubing, did she?" He glanced into the house. "Have you talked to Delores? Mrs. Alvarez? Of course, she must have called you."

"Yes," Blane jumped in. "It was Mrs. Alvarez who found your aunt. She called nine-one-one."

"Who is Mrs. Alvarez?" Ryan asked, adding another name to his notepad and wondering about the need for oxygen. He hadn't seen an oxygen tank or tubing near the woman.

"Our housekeeper. She lives in the basement." Dr. Porter pointed to the windows in a rockwork basement to the side of the porch. "I don't understand. If she was here, how did my aunt fall?"

Blane pulled out his notepad. "Mrs. Alvarez stated she was down in the basement, preparing lunch. She said if the woman called out she wouldn't have heard because today was laundry day. The washer and dryer are in the basement as well."

Dr. Porter nodded. "Yes, they aren't new machines. They make quite a racket." He settled his gaze on Blane. "How is she? Can I see Delores?"

"Not yet. I'd like to speak with her when I finish speaking to you." Ryan tapped his notepad. "If this Jeffery was here when you left and should have been here with your aunt, where is he now?"

"I've no idea. As far as I've discerned from conversations with him and my aunt, they talk in the morning, her telling him about her life, and then he writes it up in the afternoon while she rests. She reads what he wrote that day after dinner, marking changes. I know I've heard him typing in his room at night when I've gone to bed." Dr. Porter pulled his phone from a holster on his belt. "I can call him and see where he's at if that will help."

"I'll take the number and call him when I'm through speaking to Mrs. Alvarez." Ryan read the number on the doctor's phone, jotting it down in his notes.

"Where were you when Blane called you?"

The man's pale face should have caught on fire as bright red as it turned.

"I know you weren't at your office. Shandra was there waiting for you. She had an appointment." Ryan studied the man. What could he have been doing that would turn him that many shades of red?

"I was having lunch."

"Alone?"

The man's jaw moved slightly as if he were chewing on the words to say.

"No. But I prefer not to bring my lunch partner into this." The tips of the doctor's ears were almost purple.

"I see. Is she married?" Ryan had discovered the last couple of years working as a detective for a small community, there was a lot of bed hopping.

"No! I would never try to win the affections of a married woman." Now the color in his face matched the anger in his eyes.

"I see. Then I see no reason why you shouldn't disclose her name." Ryan poised his pen over his notepad.

"She…We haven't told anyone." He nodded his head toward Officer Blane.

Ryan pulled his camera out of the backpack he'd left inside the front door. "Blane, why don't you start taking photos."

The young officer's face lit up. "Yes, sir."

"Don't move anything and take photos from all directions." Ryan returned to the doctor. He said in a lowered voice, "This an under-aged girl?" He didn't think the proper doctor would do something that morally wrong, but he had to ask.

"No! I'd never do anything so disgusting." Porter glared at him. "But she's in her twenties and

I'm, well almost fifteen years older than her. I've known her since I moved here, but it wasn't until last December that I realized how special she was." He glanced back at Blane. "I don't want this getting around town. I promised I'd let her tell her parents when she was ready."

"I won't ask her name now, but you may have to tell me later." Ryan had a gut feeling the man wasn't making this story up just to have a whale of an alibi. In the years he'd known the doctor as a ME, Dr. Porter had never done anything that wasn't strictly by the book. The young woman must be really something for him to be dating her, considering the doctor felt the age difference was a problem.

"Can you tell me where you were? Maybe someone saw your car."

"Am I a suspect?" He crossed his arms, closing himself to any more open confidences.

"Everyone who knew her is a suspect until I rule them out." Ryan tipped his head toward the doctor's car. "Where were you?"

"The car was parked at the Chalet Motel." His eyes narrowed. "But that's not where I was. It's where I park when I visit my friend's place."

"I'll check that out." Ryan walked into the house, ducking under the tape. He said to Blane, "Finish up the photos and keep him out there. The ME should be showing up any minute, along with a couple of deputies. I'll be down in the basement interviewing Mrs. Alvarez. Call me when they all arrive."

"Yes, sir." Blane held the camera in one hand and placed the other one on the handle of his revolver.

Ryan did another quick scan of the body as he walked by. To most people, it appeared to be an elderly woman fell down the stairs. However, the marks he'd witnessed on her body and her lack of oxygen paraphernalia had him thinking otherwise.

He found the stairs to the basement and descended. At the bottom, in a small entry of sorts, he stopped and listened. The sound was that of someone sniffling.

To his right was a heavy door, to his left was an open doorway with bright light. He went left and stepped into a large industrial looking kitchen. A Hispanic woman with gray streaks in her braided black hair sat at a table, her head in her hands, crying.

"Mrs. Alvarez?" he asked, in a normal voice.

Her head snapped up. Her eyes were swollen from crying. "Sí, I am Mrs. Alvarez. And you?"

"I'm Detective Ryan Greer with the Weippe County Sheriff's Department. I'd like to ask you some questions about before and after you found Mrs. Narvel." He walked up to the table and put a hand on the back of a chair. "Mind if I have a seat?"

"Sit." She stood and bustled over to the gas stove. A large enamelware coffee pot sat on a lit burner. She poured two cups of coffee and sat back down.

"I did not hear anything. I was down here, making Mrs. Narvel's lunch. The washing machine and drying machine, they were making much noise." Tears glistened in her eyes. She waved to a tray sitting on the end of the table. "I sent her lunch up on the dummy and went to get her and found…" Her bottom lipped quivered.

"Were you the only one in the house?" He wanted to take her mind away from the sight, even though he still had some questions about the body.

"Sí. Mr. Jeffery told me at breakfast he would be going out for lunch." She shrugged. "I do not know when he left. I was down here."

"Did anyone visit this morning?"

Her body froze a second before she shook her head. "No. No one."

He put a question mark beside visitors.

"When you found Mrs. Narvel, how did you know she was dead?"

"She no breathe. I put a hand on her back. It didn't move." Her hand sitting on the table beside the coffee cup trembled.

"Did you touch or move anything?"

"No. I call nine-one-one. I tell lady, Mrs. Narvel fall and is dead." She sniffed. "I waited on the porch until the officer came."

Chapter Three

Shandra wasn't ready to leave Huckleberry. The best place in town for gossip was Ruthie's. Her friend had the only burger joint that was open year around. It was where the locals liked to visit and eat Ruthie's great burgers and shakes. Once the tourists discovered the café, they were repeat customers.

She parked in front of the diner, leaving the windows down half way. Sheba could entertain herself with the smells and not roast in the April sunshine.

"Shandra, it's good to see you," Ruthie said, coming out from behind the counter and giving her a hug.

"Careful, I'm in town to see Dr. Porter. I can't seem to shake this cough." As if on cue, she went into a coughing fit. Hiding her mouth in the crook of her arm, she tried to avoid spreading her germs.

"Take a seat. I'll bring you a cup of hot tea with lots of honey." Ruthie pivoted and disappeared into the kitchen.

Shandra took her usual spot where she could see everyone who entered and the people walking by outside. There were only three other people in the diner. A thirtyish man and woman she'd never seen before, and Elbert, the elderly gas station attendant from the Jiffy Mart on the way to the ski resort.

Elbert shoved his plate and bowl to the center of the counter where he was sitting, placed a bill under the edge of the plate, and stood. He glanced around, saw her, and grinned. He shuffled over to her table. "I heard you coughing when you come in. Take care of yerself, young lady."

"I will. Thank you." She smiled up at the grizzled, hunched old man. "Is this your lunch break?"

"Yep. I like Ruthie's soups." He smiled, showing a mouth with missing teeth.

"She's a good cook." Shandra said, wondering about the old man's history in the town.

"And a nice lady. Like you. See you next time you need gas." He raised a hand in a wave and shuffled to the door.

Ruthie brought out a small tea pot, cup, and jar of honey. She placed the items on the table and slid onto the bench across from Shandra.

"Did you hear about Dr. Porter's aunt?" Ruthie asked.

"Yes. I was at the clinic when they called

looking for him." She wasn't going to add she'd followed Ryan to the house. "I don't know that much about her. Do you?"

"Before her breathing became so bad, she would come in here every Saturday afternoon for a shake. Vanilla. I told her she could make one herself at home, but she said she liked coming here. It reminded her of when she was a girl." Ruthie shook her head. "That woman and her husband pretty much built this town. There was nothing here but that house they lived in, a gas station, grocery store, and post office when they moved here. Mr. Narvel brought in the ski resort and moved the town into the twenty-first century." She nodded toward the couple. "That guy is living at the Narvel house, writing Mrs. Narvel's memoirs."

Shandra stopped stirring honey into her tea and watched the couple. "Really. Does he know about Mrs. Narvel?"

"From the way the two of them have been sitting, staring at one another, I don't think so." Ruthie stood. "The woman looks kind of familiar but she's not from around here." She shook her head. "Look at them. They're happy. I'm not going to tell them." She walked into the kitchen.

Shandra picked up her tea pot and cup of tea and wandered over to the counter, plopping down on the stool closest to the booth where the couple sat. She sipped her tea and tried to pick up bits of the conversation.

"I still can't believe you talked her into letting me stay in the house," the woman said.

"It was easy. Listening to her tell her life story I could tell she misses family. With you being her granddaughter, there was no way she'd let you stay anywhere else." The man slid out of the bench. "Come on, she should be finished with lunch, you can visit with her before she rests."

Shandra remained at the counter as the two left the building. From the way the man talked, he didn't know Mrs. Narvel was dead.

Ruthie sauntered out of the kitchen, "I could have sworn I left you in that booth over yonder." She pointed with the rag in her hand toward the booth where the honey pot sat.

"Did you know Mrs. Narvel had a granddaughter?" Shandra didn't care her friend had just called her a snoop.

"No, she doesn't. The only relative she's ever talked about is Dr. Porter. She worried about him because he has the same genetics that caused his grandfather and her brother to die at the age of fifty." Ruthie sat down on the stool next to Shandra. "She asked him to come live with her after he finished his schooling and internship to help her with her illness and to save money for his research to discover how to live longer than his male relatives."

"Maybe that's where he was?" A thought struck Shandra. "Where does he work on this research?"

"In special rooms in the back of the clinic. Mrs. Narvel had the clinic built when Dr. Porter moved here. Otherwise, we had to go to Warner for doctor's appointments and any emergency." Ruthie rubbed at something on the counter top. "Mrs. Narvel and her husband have been benefactors to this town for a lot of years."

Shandra nodded, but her mind was circling. If his research lab was in the clinic, then he hadn't been working on that at the time of his aunt's death. Where had he been? And did he know he had a cousin?

~*~

Ryan walked up the stairs after talking with Mrs. Alvarez as the ME and deputies from Warner walked up on the porch. He joined Dr. Roswell, Patrol Captain Leeland, and Deputy Ron Trapp. "Captain, I didn't expect to see you here."

"You requested two deputies and Gerald was off today." Leeland nodded at the body. "Accident?"

"I don't think so, but Dr. Roswell and the state coroner will be able to tell us for sure." He nodded to Trapp. "I haven't had time to check around outside for anything that looks out of place. From the statements so far, the deceased and the housekeeper were the only people here at the time."

Leeland's attention riveted on him. "Housekeeper. Did she hear anything?"

"No, she claims to have been in the basement kitchen making the woman's lunch and doing laundry. She discovered the body when she was delivering the lunch."

"Is she telling the truth?" Leeland asked.

"About her actions, yes. But she's hiding

something. When I asked about any visitors, she hesitated, then said no." He wrote the woman's name on a page in his notebook and tore it out. "Why don't you check her out."

The captain nodded and headed back to a county car to contact the department and get information.

Ryan turned his attention to the Medical Examiner checking the body. "What do you think?"

"I think you're correct in thinking this may not have been an accident. There are bruises on her wrists that indicate someone held her tight enough to leave marks. The person had long slender fingers. As for cause of death…that will have to come from the coroner. I can't be conclusive by just looking at her." He stood, filled out a form, and handed it to Ryan. "She can be bagged and sent to Coeur d'Alene."

As if his ears were burning, Maxwell Treat, the son part of Treat and Son Mortuary, ducked under the crime scene tape, pulling a gurney behind him.

"This is a darn shame. Poor Doc Porter is all torn up." Treat stopped at the body and shook his head. Treat was the ebony to Dr. Porter's ivory complexion. His dark skin was stretched over a tall, wide, muscular body. He looked more like an athlete than a mortician, ambulance driver, and search and rescue volunteer.

Ryan handed the signed death certificate to Treat. "Yeah, he said this is his only relative."

"That's for sure. After Mr. Narvel died, Mrs. Narvel was always saying she couldn't wait for her nephew to get out of school and come join her. He was all the family she had left." Treat unzipped the body bag and placed it on the floor by the deceased woman.

"Make sure she goes straight to the state coroner's." Ryan headed to the door.

"This ain't an accident?" Treat asked.

"I'm afraid not," he said over his shoulder as a car pulled up behind the county rigs.

Treat had the forethought to pull up on the lawn with the ambulance. In this small community, he drove the ambulance to make ends meet since there were usually not enough bodies to lay to rest in Huckleberry to support two family members. And it made sense, as with this case, where the body would go to the coroner, then back to the mortuary.

A man and woman got out of the car and hurried up to the porch. Dr. Porter stepped in front of the man. "Where were you? If you had been here this wouldn't have happened." The doctor's frustration and grief gave his long angular face the effect of a caricature of a skeleton.

"What are you talking about?" the new arrival asked.

Ryan joined them on the porch. "I'm Detective Ryan Greer with the Weippe County Sheriff's Office. Who are you?"

"Why are all these police here?" the woman asked.

"I need both your names," Ryan ordered.

"Jeffery Holmes. Mrs. Narvel's biographer."

"Genie Tapfer, Mrs. Narvel's granddaughter."

"Her what? That's a lie!" Dr. Porter said, taking a position in front of the woman. "My aunt never had a child."

"It's a secret that was coming out in her book," Holmes said, a slimy smirk on his face.

A gut intuition that the man was passing this girl off as the granddaughter had Ryan asking, "When did you find out about a granddaughter?" He studied Holmes to confirm his thoughts.

"End of December or the first of January. Whenever we came to her teen years and how she'd become pregnant by a family member, but no one believed her. They sent her off to a convent where she had the baby, and it was given up for adoption." He smiled and tapped Dr. Porter in the chest with a finger. "She didn't want you to know. After all these years, she figured it would be insane to try and find the baby she gave up. So, there was no sense in you finding out until the book came out."

Dr. Porter's glare didn't seem to dampen the writer's glee at knowing something the woman's own nephew didn't know.

"Then how did Miss Tapfer end up here?" Ryan asked, putting himself between the doctor and the writer.

"I did some digging and discovered her mother, but by the time I found Mrs. Tapfer, she had passed. Cancer took her." Holmes gestured with his hand for the young woman to say something.

"After mom passed, I couldn't go through her things right away, then two months ago, I finally dug through the boxes I'd packed her belongings in when her landlord said the apartment had to be cleaned out. I came across her birth certificate. It didn't make sense. The mother's name wasn't the name of the grandmother I knew. When I asked my grandmother, she said mom was adopted. It had never been mentioned. I asked where she was adopted from and began following paper trails. I ended up with Mrs. Narvel as possibly being my grandmother." She smiled. "She asked me to move in with her while we discovered if we're related."

"When did you speak to her?" Ryan asked.

"Last night, when I arrived in town. I called her from the motel, told her who I was and who I thought she was. She was very kind and asked me to come by this afternoon with my proof and to stay with her."

"If you talked with Mrs. Narvel, how come you are arriving with Mr. Holmes?" Ryan asked.

The woman's cheeks reddened. "Mrs. Narvel sent Mr. Holmes to come get me."

Holmes jumped in. "Yes. This morning during our usual recording time, she told me about the phone call and asked that I go around and check on the woman to see if she was legitimate and bring her back this afternoon." He stretched on his toes, peering into the house. "Where is Mrs. Narvel?"

The gurney and body bag covering the older woman pushed under the crime scene tape with Treat following behind.

"Who is that?" Miss Tapfer asked.

"Aunt Gladys," Dr. Porter said, his voice barely loud enough to hear.

"It can't be!" Miss Tapfer crumpled into Mr. Holmes' arms.

Chapter Four

Shandra left Ruthie's, slogged through the grocery store, coughing and blowing her nose, to get a few ingredients to add to dinner, and caught herself dozing off twice on the drive home. Her body retaliated from the long day in town by running out of energy. She left the Jeep parked in front of the house after carrying in the bag of groceries. It took all her effort to put the cold foods in the refrigerator. Using the last of her energy, she made a cup of tea and lay down on the couch to rest. She had an hour before she had to make dinner.

After two sips of tea, she set the cup on the table and let her eyelids flutter down. It was a restless—half aware and half dream—sleep that had her feeling as if she were up making dinner.

Ella sat at the counter watching. Shandra turned to her grandmother. The woman always appeared wispy in her dreams. This time she was all white, like a cloud. "Why are you visiting?" Shandra asked, stirring a pot of soup.

Her grandmother pointed to the soup.

Shandra looked down. Funny, she didn't have alphabet noodles, yet there in the middle of the pot was a scramble of six letters. She peered at the letters until they spelled the word "Family".

"Whose family? Mine? Ryan's?" She glanced back up and Lil stood by the counter.

"Lil, what are you doing here?"

"Your Jeep has been running in front of the house for an hour. You coming or going?" the feisty older woman asked.

Her voice was clear, loud, and jarring. Shandra shook herself awake and discovered she, nor Lil, were in the kitchen. The couch was under her, and Sheba sat on the floor beside her head.

"I left the Jeep running?" She thought. "I'm sure I turned it off."

"I just turned it off. Here's the keys." Lil held out her hand, dangling the keys to the Jeep and the house. Today, the woman wore a purple long-sleeved cotton shirt, jeans, and her usual purple ball cap. Her short white hair stuck out like stalagmites from under the edge of the cap.

Shandra sat up. She started coughing.

"That doctor give you anything for your cough and cold?" Lil picked up the tea cup. Felt it and headed to the kitchen.

"No. I had to reschedule. His aunt died."

Lil hurried back into the main room with a

steaming cup. "Gladys Narvel is dead?" She set the cup on the table in front of Shandra and sunk down on the nearest chair. "That woman has been the pillar of this community for years."

"You knew her?" Shandra picked up the cup and sipped the sweet soothing warmth.

"Back when her husband was still alive, the two of them attended every community function and were on every committee. Pappy respected the Narvels, but he'd heard rumors that Mr. Narvel had shady ways of making money." She shook her head. "I don't think there was a person around here who believed it."

"Do you know what kind of shady way?" Her mind was becoming clearer. It was a long shot that someone would be retaliating for a bad deal this many years later.

"No. Like I said, it was just a rumor. No facts. And look at all the good they did for this town. I'm surprised the city council didn't change the name of the town to Narville." She cringed. "Maybe that's why. Not near as inviting as Huckleberry."

"I agree." Shandra swung her legs over the side of the couch. "I need to get dinner started. Thank you for turning the Jeep off. I was too tired to park it in the barn." She stood, and the room spun.

Lil shot to her feet, grabbing her arm. "You sure you shouldn't stay lying down? Your hot as a microwaved burrito and pale as the doc."

Shandra slumped back down on the couch. "I told Ryan I'd have dinner ready."

"He's a big boy. I'm sure he can fend for

himself. Go back to sleep. I'll put the Jeep away."

This was one time she didn't have the energy to argue with Lil. Her eyelids dropped and her world went dark.

Ryan and the captain checked out the second floor and snapped photos of anything that looked out of place. If there had been a struggle, it had either been covered up or had been brief. The one thing that bugged him was the lack of an oxygen tank with the victim. From the machine in the woman's bedroom and the coiled up clear tubing, she must have had a portable tank for moving about the house. But after searching all the rooms on all the floors except the fourth, which he'd found locked, neither he nor Leeland could find a portable tank.

Before they'd started the search of the house, Miss Tapfer had regained consciousness. She, Mr. Holmes, and Dr. Porter all sat on the porch waiting under the watchful gaze of Officer Blane.

Ryan walked out onto the porch. "Miss Tapfer, you may have Mr. Holmes take you back to your motel," he said, dismissing the two.

"But I was asked by my grandmother to stay here," the woman sputtered.

"Under the circumstances, I believe it would be best if you remained in a motel." Ryan had noted anger brewing on Dr. Porter's face. He added. "I also suggest you remain in town until this is cleared up."

"Am I a suspect?" she asked, moving closer to

Mr. Holmes.

Ryan's first instinct about the two of them knowing each other better than they were letting on struck again. "No, at this time you aren't a suspect. But I like to keep everyone involved in a case close, so I can ask them questions."

"Mr. Holmes, I suggest you take Miss Tapfer back to her motel." Ryan already had the man's number from Dr. Porter but he didn't want the man to know. "Could you give me your phone number in case I have any questions for you?"

"Of course, I want to help in any way I can," said Holmes before he rattled off his number.

When the man and woman were in the car, Ryan turned his attention to Dr. Porter. "I have a few more questions I'd like to ask both you and Mrs. Alvarez."

The doctor nodded.

"Blane, would you ask Mrs. Alvarez to join Dr. Porter and myself in the parlor, please." Ryan pulled down the crime scene tape. "I think we've discovered all we're going to get from here."

Dr. Porter walked hesitantly through the doorway, his gaze on the carpet at the bottom of the stairs. The pattern of the rug hid the small smears of blood from the lacerations the woman had received from the tumble.

Ryan turned to Captain Leeland. "Captain, you can go home, but I'd like Ron to stay in the Huckleberry area for the rest of his shift." Ryan watched Dr. Porter and the housekeeper hug when they met at the door to the parlor.

"I'll inform Trapp." The captain headed to his SUV, stopping and conversing with the deputy before driving off.

Ryan entered the parlor. The housekeeper sat on the edge of a small chair. Dr. Porter stood by the fireplace. A painting of the deceased woman and a man ten years older than her hung over the mantel.

"What can you tell me about the oxygen devices Mrs. Narvel used?" he asked, taking a seat on a chair. He opened his notepad.

"She had the oxygen concentrator in her room with enough tubing to move about her room and use the bathroom" Dr. Porter nodded to the hallway. "There was another concentrator in the closet at the end of the hall that allowed her mobility on this floor. A person comes in once a week from Warner to check fittings, and make sure everything is running as it should."

"What about when she went up and down the stairs or went to town?" Ryan watched the housekeeper.

"She had a small portable canister she used for the stairs or when she left the house. That was also replaced and checked when the man from Warner came over." Dr. Porter's eyes widened. "When I glanced in the door, I didn't see her canister. Was she laying on it?"

Ryan asked Mrs. Alvarez, "Do you remember seeing the canister when you found Mrs. Narvel?"

The woman's eyes widened, "No. I did not see the oxygen machine." She placed a hand in front of her mouth. "She could not walk down the stairs without it."

Dr. Porter strode over and stood in front of Ryan. "What are you saying? Was this not an accident?"

"My preliminary investigation is pointing toward homicide."

"No!" Mrs. Alvarez shook her head. She mumbled in Spanish and moved her right hand in the Catholic sign of the cross.

Dr. Porter sat on the sofa as if he'd deflated. "Who would want to kill Aunt Gladys?" He stared at Ryan as if the answer was written on his forehead.

"That's what I plan to find out." He slid forward in his chair. "Can you think of anyone who would have a reason to want your aunt dead?"

"No one." Dr. Porter stared at the painting. "She's, was, a pillar of the community. She gives, gave, to all the charities. At one time, she was on all the committees. I can't think of anyone who doesn't, didn't, like her."

"Sí, Mrs. Narvel have many friends," the housekeeper said.

"Someone had a reason to kill her."

Dr. Porter flinched at his blunt statement.

"What about this woman, Genie Tapfer, saying she's your aunt's granddaughter. Had you heard anything over the years that would give you reason to believe her claim?" Ryan hadn't observed a resemblance between the two. She was colorful to Dr. Porter's monotonous bland coloring.

"I have never heard a word about my aunt

having a child or giving one up." The doctor shot to his feet. "I want to see this memoir Jeffrey has been writing."

Ryan stood, putting himself between the man and the door. "While this is your house, you can't go into his room and take his manuscript. It's his property." A thought came to him. "But since this woman showed up on the same day as your aunt's death, claiming to be her granddaughter, I may be able to get a warrant for a copy of the manuscript and the tapes. To see if we can't discover if Miss Tapfer is a relation or not."

Mrs. Alvarez stood. "I will fix your dinner."

"No. Don't bother. I'm not hungry." Doctor Porter sat back down and stared at the portrait.

The housekeeper nodded and left the room.

"Do you have anyone you need to call?" Ryan asked, glancing at his watch. He was going to be late for dinner. Luckily, Shandra understood the fluctuating hours of his job.

"I—I want to call my friend, but she's at work. I hate to bother her there." He dropped his head in his hands.

He shouldn't feel compassion for a person who was still a suspect, but in the last two years he'd met the doctor on several occasions and had the feeling the man didn't have many friends. "Hey, you want to join Shandra and I for dinner at her place?"

He glanced up. "I wouldn't be good company." His gaze traveled around the room. "But I really don't want to stay here. I wish my friend wasn't working." He sucked in air and made a grab for the phone on his belt. "I haven't even had time to tell her…"

He'd never seen the always professional doctor look so lost and unsure.

"How about I give you a ride out to Shandra's. She has a guest room. You can stay the night there and figure out the rest in the morning."

Gratitude shone in the man's light blue eyes. "You sure you won't get in trouble for this? I have a pretty good suspicion I'm a suspect if you think this wasn't accidental."

"I'm not harboring you, Shandra is. It's her house. If I happen to be living there too, well, we'll worry about it when the time comes."

Dr. Porter stood. "I've always loved this house, but tonight, I just want to get away from it."

"Grab what you need for overnight." Ryan walked out into the hall.

"I have a bag in the car. You know, in case I have to spend the night at the clinic." Dr. Porter went over to a box on the wall and pressed a button.

"Sí?" Mrs. Alvarez's voice replied.

"Mrs. Alvarez, I won't be here this evening. I'll see you tomorrow." Dr. Porter didn't wait for a reply, he walked to the front door, waited for Ryan to exit and pulled it shut, locking the large brass handle.

Porter pulled his doctor bag, laptop bag, and a duffle out of the back seat of his car and walked over to Ryan's Tahoe.

Once they were both seated in the vehicle, Ryan headed to town. He called Sheriff Oldham, asking him to start a warrant for Gladys Narvel's memoirs. He also called Deputy Trapp to let him know where he was going.

"Thanks. I really don't think I could have figured out what to do. Aunt Gladys has been more like a mother to me. I-I still can't believe she's gone." Dr. Porter propped an elbow on the door and leaned his head into his hand.

"Shandra won't mind. Maybe you can diagnose her. You missed her appointment today." He was joking but glanced over and the man nodded his head.

Three miles out of Huckleberry a beeping started. Porter looked at his phone. Relief washed over his taut features.

"Hello. Sorry. I know. You shouldn't have heard from someone else. I've just been numb." He listened. "I'm not home. I couldn't stand being there tonight." He listened some more. "I didn't want to bother you at work. And your parents…" He nodded. "She didn't die of natural causes." He rubbed a hand over his face. "I'm riding with Detective Greer to Shandra Higheagle's house." He shook his head. "Why? I don't know. I knew you were working and I…I couldn't think straight." He sighed. "Thank you. I'll see you tomorrow. Bye."

"Your girlfriend you won't name?" Ryan asked.

"Yeah, she heard about my aunt at work and wanted to know why I didn't call her." He shoved the phone back in his phone holster and shrugged. "This is one of the reasons I have had few female friends. I'm not a good communicator."

Ryan chuckled. "Aren't we all when it comes to women."

They rode the rest of the way to Shandra's in silence.

Pulling up to the house, Ryan noted how quiet and dark the interior looked. He hadn't called ahead to tell Shandra he was bringing a guest. He was sure, knowing how inquisitive she'd been earlier in the day, the guest would be welcome.

Chapter Five

Shandra woke to Sheba's happy bark. The dog's usual deep bark was an octave higher. She stood on her back feet, looking out the front door window that was high enough for a person to peer out, not usually a dog.

"Is that Ryan?" She sat up and someone started tap dancing in her head. "Oh!" The dog and the dancing feet were more than she could bear. "Sheba, please, knock it off."

The front door opened. Ryan usually came in the back. But it had to be Ryan, otherwise Sheba wouldn't be so excited.

"Ryan?" she asked, opening her eyes.

"Yeah. Why is it so dark in here?"

The lights went on, and she covered her eyes. "Oh!"

"Are you feeling worse?" Ryan's voice was

near her head.

"Yeah. My head is pounding…I was—"

A hand felt her forehead. "She's burning up." Ryan pulled the blanket down from her face. "Dr. Porter's here. Let him take a look."

"Dr. Porter? Why?"

"We'll discuss it later."

Ryan disappeared from view and Dr. Porter's face appeared.

"Shandra, put this under your tongue." His voice was calm and void of emotion.

She tried to stare at him to see what he was feeling, but the harder she tried to focus his blurry image, the more her head pounded.

He removed the thermometer from her mouth. "You have a fever. Let me look at your ears, nose, and throat."

She felt the slight invasion of the scope he used to look into her ear and nose.

"Open wide and say, ahh."

She opened her mouth, he placed the depressor on her tongue, and she about gagged.

"You look like a case of strep. I have a sample antibiotic in my bag. You can start it tonight. I'll give Ryan a prescription to get you more from the pharmacy." He patted her shoulder and reached in his bag.

Ryan appeared by her side with a glass of cold water. Dr. Porter handed him two small packages. "Take this, and I'll put you to bed."

"Why are there three pills?" she asked, plucking the two white and one colored capsule from his hand. "I don't want to go to bed. I want to know why Dr. Porter is here and what you learned." She swallowed the pills and placed the cup on the table.

"One was the antibiotic and the other two were for your pain and fever." Ryan scooped her up in his arms. "I'll be right back, Doc."

"I don't want to go to bed."

"That's too bad. You won't be able to remain awake if you stay on the couch so you might as well get plenty of sleep." Ryan placed her on the bed. "I brought Dr. Porter here because I felt sorry for him. Losing his only relative has been a shock."

"You're such a softy. How did you ever become a cop?" Shandra put a hand on his face and tried to see his emotions through her fever haze.

He pulled the covers on the bed down. "Get in. I'll fill you in on everything when you're more lucid." He kissed her forehead, turned out the light, and left the room.

"Looks like it's just you and me, Ella."

~*~

Ryan was smiling at how childlike Shandra became when she was ill as he entered the main room. Dr. Porter sat on the couch, staring into the flames of the gas fireplace. Sheba lay at the man's feet, her big brown eyes drooping in sympathy.

"I'm going to make a sandwich. You want anything?" he asked, stopping in front of the other man.

"No. I-I can't fathom she's gone. She had another ten to fifteen years." He ran a hand through his hair, standing it on end. "I'd hoped she'd be alive to see I made it past fifty."

Ryan sat down on the chair. "Past fifty? What do you mean?"

Dr. Porter's lips twisted in a snide smile. "My lack of pigmentation. It's an inherited gene that also takes the male heirs lives by the age of fifty. I've been working on research that I believe will help counteract the gene's attack on my organs." He held up two fingers a millimeter apart. "I'm this close to getting it right." He lowered his hand and sighed. "I wanted Aunt Gladys to see what her faith in me had accomplished. That the Porter line might continue past me."

"Her faith in you?" Ryan stood, his growling stomach needed fed.

"She's been paying for all the research. Even paid for my medical schooling. That's why I moved here to help her and continue the research I started while in school and interning." Dr. Porter leaned back, resting his head on the back of the leather couch. "I did all of it for her. She hated losing her father and brother so young."

"What happens now? You'll still have funds to continue the research, won't you?" The man was the sole heir, unless Miss Tapfer's claim was substantiated.

"Yes, Aunt Gladys left everything to me as the only living heir." His eyes opened. "I don't know what will happen if that woman's claims are valid."

"And you knew nothing of her claim before this afternoon?" He didn't like thinking Dr. Porter killed his aunt to keep his research funding, but he'd seen murders committed for a lot less.

"I knew my aunt received a call last night, but she didn't tell me anything about it. This morning she was more animated than usual when I left for work. I put it off as being excited about whatever she was going to recite to Jeffery." He scowled. "I didn't like the idea when she told me she was looking for someone to write her memoirs. But after watching her excitement over telling her story, I decided it couldn't hurt." His face crumpled. "And now she's dead."

Ryan shuffled his feet a moment then mumbled. "I'm going to make sandwiches." He headed into the kitchen. It was either the mention of sandwiches or the room he entered, Sheba arrived within seconds of his opening the refrigerator door.

"You hungry too?" He tossed her a slice of cheese. Drool slid out the sides of her mouth as she watched him prepare two ham and cheese sandwiches. He grabbed a bag of chips and returned to the main room.

Dr. Porter was once again staring into the fire.

"Here's a sandwich and chips in case you get hungry." Ryan grabbed his food and sat back in the chair.

Sheba's nose spun from pointing at his sandwich to the window. She woofed and ambled to the door.

Ryan rose and joined her. A compact red car sat next to his SUV. The inside light went on as the driver's side door opened. The long body and wavy dark hair belonged to a person he knew. What was Miranda Aducci doing at Shandra's this hour of the night?

"Sit!" he ordered Sheba and opened the door.

"Where is Alex?" she asked, striding up to the door on her long legs.

"Alex?" He had a notion she meant Dr. Porter and that this was the woman the doctor was trying to protect.

"Dr. Porter. He's still here, isn't he?"

Before Ryan could answer the question, she pushed by him and headed straight for the couch.

Dr. Porter, Alex, sat up. "What are you doing here?"

Miranda sat on the couch beside him, her palm cupping his face. "You are hurting. I'm here for you."

Alex wrapped his arms around the woman and buried his face in her long hair.

Ryan ducked into the kitchen. The moment looked private, and he didn't want to interrupt. He could ask Miranda if the doctor had been with her when he received the call. His brain did a fast retracing of the events. If Dr. Porter had been with her, she would have already known something had happened to his aunt. Wouldn't she have come with him to the house given her quick arrival after he told her what had happened and where he was?

He grabbed three beers out of the refrigerator and headed back into the room.

Dr. Porter's head was resting on Miranda's ample chest as her arm curled around his shoulders.

"How about a beer?" Ryan asked, placing two of the bottles on the burl table in front of the couch. He leaned back in the chair across from the two. "I take it you're the woman Alex refused to name when I asked where he was when he received the call about his aunt."

Miranda's eyes widened. She turned her gaze on the man, sitting up and reaching for the beer. "You knew she was dead when you left me and didn't say anything?"

Alex twisted the top off the beer and handed it to the woman. "I didn't know she was dead. Officer Blane said there had been an accident."

Miranda took the beer but didn't drink. Her eyes narrowed on the man next to her. "But you found out as soon as you arrived and didn't even call me? I thought we'd become close. Close enough to help carry the other's burdens."

Ryan felt compelled to help out his fellow male. "We were questioning him and the others."

"Others? Who else was there? Oh, Mrs. Alvarez. And that writer. He didn't look shook up tonight." She sipped the beer.

"You saw Mr. Holmes tonight? Where?" Ryan jumped on her comment. If she'd seen him he had to be at the restaurant.

"At the restaurant. He and some woman. A blonde, in her thirties, pretty. They were smiling and holding hands. I was wondering how he met someone if he was always writing."

Dr. Porter sat up. "He and the woman were holding hands?"

"Yes." She glanced back and forth between Dr. Porter and Ryan.

"That woman showed up at the house with Jeffery when they brought Aunt Gladys out of the house." Dr. Porter grasped Miranda's hand. "She said she was my aunt's granddaughter."

Miranda shook her head. "Mrs. Narvel never said anything about having a child, let alone a granddaughter. Momma would know. Her mother worked for Mrs. Narvel's family in Portland. It was Mrs. Narvel who suggested Momma and Poppa start up a restaurant here. She and her husband loaned the money to start the business."

Ryan pulled out his notepad. "Tomorrow, I'd like to speak with your mother." He jotted down her name.

"I'll tell her you will be coming by the restaurant before it opens." Miranda sipped her beer and scanned the room. "Where is Shandra?"

"She's sick. I put her to bed."

The young woman smiled before her lips curved into a sad frown. "Having been caught up in the murders last year with her, I bet she isn't happy to be sick when another death has occurred."

"She wasn't." Ryan waved his half empty bottle between the two sitting on the couch. "You two spending the night? I'm beat. I need to get some sleep."

Miranda set the empty bottle on the table and stood. "No. I'm taking him back to my place. Come on, Alex."

Dr. Porter stood. "Thank you for taking me

away from the house. I'll stay with Miranda tonight and face it in the morning." He held out a hand.

Ryan shook. "No problem. I could tell you were devastated. Take care of him," he said to the young woman.

"I will." She grasped the doctor's hand and led him to the door.

"These are my bags," he said, reaching down and grabbing all three handles. He glanced back at Ryan. "You'll let me know when you get that manuscript and what you learn?"

"Yes. I will." He walked to the door and watched the couple walk to her car. Miranda was a good six inches taller than the doctor and so vibrant and full of live, she was the opposite of the man she cared for.

When he could no longer see the taillights, he pulled out his phone and dialed the Weippe Sherriff's Department. Charles Wyland, the night dispatch operator, answered.

"Charles, would you leave a note for Cathleen. I need information on a woman, mid-thirties, name of Genie Tapfer. I'm not sure where she came from yet, but I hope to find out in the morning. Also, a writer named Jeffery Holmes."

"Is this in regard to the death in Huckleberry today?" Charles asked.

"Yes. The body should have made it to the coroners by now. I'll contact them in the morning and see where it is on the docket. Thanks." He hung up and pulled out his laptop. He could do the superficial digging on Jeffery Holmes. It seemed like more than a coincidence that Miss Tapfer arrived the same day Mrs. Narvel died, claiming to be her granddaughter.

Chapter Six

Shandra woke feeling as if she needed to tell someone something. The soft snoring beside her made her smile. Ryan. There was a time when she didn't think she'd ever want a man sleeping beside her, but he'd been patient. She couldn't think of anyone else she'd rather have by her side day and night.

A glance at the bedside clock had her snuggling back down in the covers. Five was too early. Ryan rose at six and would soon be moving around. Until then, she'd catch a few more minutes of sleep.

Her eyes fluttered closed. She listened to the even breathing of Ryan and soon fell into a light slumber.

Ella appeared. This time she was back up in her usual clouds. Shandra shaded her eyes, looking up. The sun was blinding. Everyone appeared white.

She blinked. No not everyone. Just Dr. Porter and Ella. A young woman peeked over the doctor's shoulder. Her face had a rich caramel color and her hair was blonde.

Shandra sat up straight. It was the girl she saw peeking around the corner of the house. She should tell Ryan before she forgot.

His breathing was deep and even. She hated waking him. A glance at the clock showed he still had forty-five minutes.

She slipped out of bed, grabbed a robe, and headed to the kitchen. She didn't shiver like yesterday, but her throat still hurt and her head only throbbed instead of pounded. Sheba's nails clicked along on the wood flooring behind her.

"Would you like an early breakfast?" she asked her furry companion.

Sheba walked in a circle, her tongue dangling from her open mouth.

"That can be arranged." Shandra poured water in the coffee maker and in the tea kettle before walking into the laundry room and feeding Sheba.

Back in the kitchen, she spotted the prescription Dr. Porter said he'd leave for her. Alongside of it in a small package was a colored pill. She read the name and decided it was another of the antibiotic sample he'd left for her to use until the prescription was filled.

Her stomach rumbled as Sheba whined at the back door. "I'm coming." Her slippers scuffed across the floor as she moved to the door, letting the dog out for her morning romp around the buildings.

The tea kettle whistled. She poured water in a cup with green tea and added a tablespoon of honey. Pulling a muffin from a container, she sat at the counter and grabbed the nearest pen, writing down *blonde woman* on the back of the prescription to help her remember to tell Ryan.

The fresh brewed aroma of coffee wafted through the room as the perking sound of the coffeemaker slowed. She inhaled the scent and sipped her tea. With the rumblings in her stomach a cup of coffee would only upset her, but the smell was enticing.

Ryan's voice reached the kitchen before he did. He walked through the door talking on his cell phone. "That's interesting. Thanks, Captain." Ryan shoved his phone into the holster on his belt and smiled.

"You look better this morning. It must have been Dr. Porter's miracle drugs." He kissed her cheek and walked over to the coffeemaker.

"At least I'm not seeing the world through a fever haze." She sipped her tea. "Why did Captain Leeland call you so early?"

"I asked him to dig into the housekeeper's background. She's clean, but her daughter has been in trouble with the law since she was sixteen." He grabbed a muffin from the container and sat down beside her. "I have a feeling the daughter was visiting her yesterday morning. She hesitated when I asked if anyone had visited."

"What does her daughter look like?" Shandra had an idea she knew who the young woman she saw might be.

"I don't know." He narrowed his eyes. "Why?"

"When I was leaving yesterday, a young woman with blonde bangs, dressed in a hoodie, blue jeans, and sneakers watched you and the others from the corner of the house."

"I was right. Mrs. Alvarez did have a visitor. I'll ask her about it this morning." He sipped his coffee.

Shandra nodded toward the three beer bottles sitting near the kitchen sink. "Did Dr. Porter need two of those to get to sleep last night?"

Ryan's grin was a bit crooked when he faced her. "You aren't going to believe who Dr. Porter has been dating and who came to get him last night."

She enjoyed the merriment dancing in his eyes and the smugness of his tone. "From the way you're acting, I'll never be able to guess."

"You're right. He and Miranda Aducci have been playing footsie since last December."

"No! Miranda? How have they kept it a secret? And why?" Shandra was happy for her friend but also curious as to why after what they'd went through together last December that Miranda didn't feel she could confide in her.

"Dr. Porter said because of the age difference Miranda was worried her parents wouldn't like it." He shook his head. "Or maybe because if Dr. Porter doesn't find a cure, he won't live past fifty."

"Do you know more about it? Ruthie didn't have the whole scoop." She had hoped Ruthie had heard wrong about the doctor.

Ryan told her about the genetics that had preordained the doctor's death.

"I hope he can go on researching and finds a cure." Shandra stood to refill her cup with hot water and grab another muffin. She was hungry but didn't feel up to cooking.

Ryan's phone buzzed. He checked the number and stepped out of the room. "Cathleen, did you get my message?"

"I did. Do you have anything more to go on for the woman? That's pretty vague." Having his big sister as the dispatcher and researcher at the Sheriff's office was helpful. However, having her know all his personal business wasn't.

"I don't know any more about her. I'll see what I can gather today. She claims to be Gladys Narvel's granddaughter. Though no one ever heard of the woman even having a child." Which reminded him of the memoirs. "Do you know if the Sheriff was able to get the warrant for the memoirs?"

"He sent it over a few minutes ago with Deputy Trapp." Cathleen's voice lowered. "You and Shandra set a date yet for a wedding?"

He blew air out between his teeth. This was the part about having a sister in his work place that bothered him. "No. We haven't. We'll let you, Mom, and Bridget know as soon as we do. Thanks." He hung up and wandered back into the kitchen.

Sheba sat at Shandra's feet waiting for a bite. Slobber hung from the sides of her mouth.

"We need to get that dog a bib," he said, filling a travel mug with coffee and scooping out two more muffins. "I have to go. The warrant for the memoirs should be in Huckleberry when I get there."

"Why do you need the memoirs?" Shandra folded the prescription and picked it up.

"That's how the writer, Jeffrey Holmes, supposedly discovered the victim had a granddaughter. I want the memoirs to see what else might have come up, and Dr. Porter wants to see what his aunt had to say about the child." He reached over to claim the white paper in Shandra's fingers.

She pulled it away. "I'll get this filled."

He moved quickly, whisking it from her grasp. "You are staying here. You're sick and don't need to be spreading your germs around Huckleberry."

Her bottom lip came out in a forced pout.

Ryan laughed. "That won't work on me. If you don't feel like working on your pottery, see what all you can dig up on the Narvels." He kissed the top of her head and left the house.

~*~

Shandra decided to get to work researching before she became tired. With another muffin, a cup of tea, and her laptop, she snuggled under a blanket on the couch and started with the newspaper archives for the weekly Huckleberry Gazette.

Being a small, family owned newspaper, it was the job of the teenagers in the family to upload back copies of the newspaper onto the website. This was one of the things she adored about Huckleberry.

While the town was small and appeared antiquated, most residents had embraced the digital revolution with gusto. It had given them access to a world outside their mountain.

The articles she pulled up all showed the couple giving money to this charity, that business. The start-up of the ski resort had articles every week for three years. It had been a large endeavor. Several times in the article it was mentioned, Mr. Narvel called his backers benevolent business men.

"There has to be a record of who these men are." She had an idea. Martha Samples, who worked at city records, was also the city's biggest gossip. Though they had been on opposite sides during the hunt to find who killed Lil's ex-boyfriend, the woman wouldn't mind helping dig up the information about the backers for the ski resort if it pertained to the latest murder.

Chapter Seven

Ryan found Deputy Ron Trapp sipping coffee and visiting with Hazel, the Huckleberry Police dispatcher.

"You have it?" he asked, walking straight toward Trapp.

"Yes. You want me to go with you?" Trapp set his cup down.

"It would be a good idea to show strength. I have a feeling Holmes isn't going to want to part with his work." Ryan pivoted and headed back out the door. "I'll meet you out there."

Within minutes, he pulled into the driveway of the old Victorian house. Dr. Porter's car and the one Holmes had driven the day before, sat in the driveway.

Trapp pulled up behind him and exited his vehicle carrying the warrant. He handed the papers to Ryan, and they both walked up to the door.

Ryan used the brass knocker, rapping three times.

Mrs. Alvarez opened the door. "Oh, Detective. I did not expect you again." The woman's gaze darted to the side as if she wanted to turn around and look at something or someone.

Believing that someone to be the daughter, in a low voice he said to Trapp, "Check around outside. Bring me anyone you see."

To the woman he said, "Yes, I'm here to serve a warrant."

"Dr. Porter has not returned since last night," the woman said, again attempting to look over her shoulder without appearing as if she were.

"This isn't for Dr. Porter. It's for Mr. Holmes." He waved the papers. "Is he up?"

"I do not know. Breakfast is laid out at seven. He should be down soon." She finally stepped back allowing him entry.

"Check the dining room, please."

"I came from there. See for yourself. He was not in the room." She motioned to the room to the right.

Ryan stepped in the doorway, noted the food on a buffet and no Jeffery Holmes. He walked over to the stairs and put a hand on the banister. "Which room is his?"

"Top of the stairs, the room on the right." She turned and headed down the hall.

He climbed the stairs. The clacking of a keyboard getting a workout came from behind the door of the room the woman had mentioned.

He rapped three times.

The clacking stopped. Holmes opened the door and stuck his head out. "What are you doing here?"

Ryan smiled and raised the warrant. "I could say the same for you. Your employer is dead. I would have thought you'd move on to another job."

Holmes stared at the paper. "Warrant? For what?"

"Your manuscript and the tapes."

The man's face paled. "You can't do this!"

"I can and I have. We believe there is information in what the deceased told you that may shed light on who killed her." Ryan put a palm on the door and shoved.

Holmes backed into the room. "I don't have anything printed out."

Ryan pointed to a section on the warrant. "Then it's a good thing our DA stated all devices, papere, and recordings of the interviews between you and Mrs. Narvel." He grinned. "It seems Mrs. Narvel and her husband helped the DA when he needed a scholarship to continue his schooling to become a lawyer."

"You can't take my computer. That's my livelihood."

"We'll only keep it long enough to get copies of your files." Ryan closed the computer and unplugged it from the wall. "Where are the recordings?"

Holmes reluctantly handed over a device the size of a cell phone. "The only thing on there are our visits."

"We'll get these back to you once the information has been copied." He started to leave then turned back. "Where is Miss Tapfer staying?"

"The Chalet Lodge motel." Holmes walked to the door. "Why do you need to talk to her?"

"Same reason I'll be back later with more questions for you. To find a murderer."

Ryan walked out of the house with the computer and recording device.

Trapp stood by his car with a young woman in a hoodie.

"Who do you have?" Ryan asked, placing the computer and recorder in his SUV.

"She's not talking. I didn't find any ID on her." Trapp nodded to the back of the house. "She came out of a back door of the basement."

Ryan stopped in front of the young woman. "Are you Dana Alvarez?"

By the widening of her eyes and the huff of disgust she emitted, he had a pretty good idea he was looking at Mrs. Alvarez's daughter.

"What are you doing here, Dana?"

"I came to see my mom." The defiance in her eyes and scowl on her face, made him think she might have been here to see her mom but it wasn't to give the older woman comfort.

"Why did you need to see your mom?" He knew from Captain Leeland's look at the mother that the daughter had been thrown out of her apartment for not paying the rent.

The woman didn't say anything.

"You hoping your mom will put you up since you no longer have a place to live?"

"How do you know that?" she spat, her eyes narrowing.

"We've been looking into your mother because of Mrs. Narvel's untimely death. You happened to pop up with a list of misdemeanors." He waited a beat but she didn't react. "I also know you were here yesterday when Mrs. Narvel died."

Her head snapped up, her eyes peered into his. "How do you know I was here?"

"For one you just acknowledged it and a witness saw you." He crossed his arms. "What were you doing here yesterday and what did you see or hear?"

"I didn't see or hear anything. I came by to see my mom." Her eyelids drooped, hiding half of her eyes. She was hiding more than her eyes from him.

"How about we march into the house and ask your mom what you were doing here?"

Hatred sparked in her dark eyes. "Go ahead. She can't tell you anything."

Ryan nodded to Trapp. The deputy grabbed her arm, and they all three walked back up to the front door. Ryan rapped the brass knocker. It took longer for someone to answer.

Mr. Holmes opened the door. "I thought you left." His gaze drifted from Ryan, to the deputy, and landed on Dana. "What's that delinquent doing here?"

"That's what we hope to ask her mother." Ryan pushed past the writer.

"Her mother?" Holmes questioned.

Ryan motioned for Trapp and the woman to step into the parlor. "Mr. Holmes, would you call down to the basement and ask Mrs. Alvarez to come to the parlor, please."

Holmes walked over to the intercom. He snapped his fingers. "You're Mrs. Alvarez's delinquent daughter. Gladys talked about you a couple of times. She's not here to bail you out again, is she?" He laughed and called the housekeeper to the parlor.

Dana glared at the writer. It appeared Holmes knew something about the young woman and the deceased.

Mrs. Alvarez stepped through the door. Her gaze landed on her daughter. "Oh! She has done nothing wrong." The housekeeper hurried over to stand by her daughter.

The young woman leaned away from her mother.

Something was going on between them.

"Deputy Trapp found this young woman coming out of the back of the basement. She refuses to tell us who she is." Ryan decided to treat the girl like a suspect until he had logical answers.

"She is my daughter, Dana. She was not causing harm. She has been staying in the basement with me." Mrs. Alvarez came to the girl's defense immediately.

"Did Mrs. Narvel know your daughter was staying in the basement?" Ryan could tell from the gleeful smile on Holmes face and the pained look on Mrs. Alvarez, the owner of the house did not know of her guest.

"I was going to tell her at lunch yesterday, but… I could not." Tears glistened in the housekeeper's eyes.

The front door opened and closed.

Ryan pivoted to the doorway.

Dr. Porter walked through. His gaze landed on Ryan first, then took in the others. "What is going on?" He placed his bags on the floor by the door and stopped beside Mrs. Alvarez.

"We were discovering who this young woman is and why she's been hanging around the house," Ryan said.

"Dana? What does he mean hanging around the house? You know what Aunt Gladys said." Dr. Porter scowled at the young woman.

"What did your aunt have to say about this young woman?" Ryan asked.

"That she wasn't allowed in the house anymore. Two months ago she stole jewelry from my aunt's room." Dr. Porter put a hand on the housekeeper's shoulder. "You know up until then, Aunt Gladys would have helped her out no matter what happened to her."

"Sí. I did not want her staying here. I do not want to lose my job. But she had nowhere to go." Mrs. Alvarez pulled a handkerchief out of her apron pocket and blew her nose.

"Was the theft reported?" Ryan asked.

"Yes. The police were able to track down the necklace and get it back to us." Dr. Porter faced

Dana. "I would have thought you'd still be in jail."

She glared at him but didn't say a word.

"Deputy, put Miss Alvarez in your car and escort her to the Huckleberry Police Department." Ryan started to follow the deputy and woman out of the room.

"Detective, please, she is trying to be a good girl," Mrs. Alvarez said.

"I only want to question her. She doesn't seem to be the talkative type. I'm hoping sitting in a room by herself for a while will loosen her lips." He nodded to the doctor to follow him.

Out on the porch, he stopped and faced the man. "That pill you gave Shandra was helping already this morning. Thanks."

He nodded. "Get the prescription filled or she'll be right back where she was."

"I will. I have Holmes' computer and recorder. After we get copies from them, I'll make sure you get a copy too. Just in case the book never gets published."

"Thanks. Do you know the cause of death yet?" His pale blue gaze bore into his.

"I'm still waiting for the coroner's report. I'll let you know what I can." Ryan started to walk off the porch and had a thought. "Who is your aunt's lawyer?"

"Yenks and Jarvis in Warner. Dalmer Jarvis was her attorney since my uncle died." Dr. Porter studied him. "You going to ask him who inherits?"

"That and a couple of other things."

"I can save you time. I was the sole beneficiary.

She wanted to make sure I had enough resources for my research." He wiped a hand across his eyes. "I didn't kill her for the money. Her emotional support meant a whole lot more to me than her financial."

Chapter Eight

Shandra straightened and leaned her head against the couch back. She'd been scrolling through the newspaper archives for hours. Her head, neck, and eyes hurt.

The back door opened and closed. Lil marched down the hall, Lewis, the orange tabby, wrapped around her neck like a fur stole. Today she had on a stripped purple shirt that matched her ball cap and jeans.

"I was going to start tilling up the garden patch and add some manure. You didn't come out to the studio, so I figured you weren't up to working today." She leaned over and placed a hand on Shandra's forehead. "You ain't as hot today. Are you still going to see the doc?"

"Tilling the garden is a good idea. No. Dr. Porter was here last night and gave me two pills and a prescription for Ryan to fill for me." Shandra set the laptop on the coffee table.

"What are you researching?"

"The Narvels. Ryan wanted to know more about their past. All I've found so far is they came from the Seattle area and put a lot of money into Weippe County and Huckleberry in particular." She picked up her cold cup of tea.

"I'll warm that for you." Lil pulled the cup from her hands and headed to the kitchen.

Sheba stood, stretched, and trotted into the kitchen.

Shandra grinned. The dog wouldn't find any treats. Lil was good to animals, but she didn't believe in treating them for no reason.

Her stomach rumbled. She pushed up off the couch as Lil came out of the kitchen.

"Sit back down. Unless you need to use the bathroom, I can get whatever you want." Lil placed the steaming cup on the coffee table and shoved her hands on her hips.

"I was hungry. There's some soup in a container in the refrigerator. If you wouldn't mind heating that up, I will make a trip to the bathroom."

When she returned, the steaming soup sat on the table beside her tea, a napkin, spoon, and thin sliced French bread. "Thank you."

"I'll be tillin'. If you need anything send Sheba out to get me." Lil spun on her heel and disappeared out the door.

Her phone played the jazz tune, *Dream a Little Dream*. She glanced at the screen and smiled. Ryan.

"Hello," she answered.

"How are you doing?" he asked.

"Better. Lil just brought me lunch. And you?"

"I'm not going to be able to bring your pills to you until tonight. I need to question someone, and I'm still waiting for the coroner's report." The apology in his voice made her smile.

"You're busy, don't worry about it. I'm feeling much better than yesterday, and I drove to town then. If you can drop the prescription off, I'll pick it up. I wanted to talk to Miranda anyway." She knew if she also told him she was going to the city recorders, he'd insist she stay home.

"I dropped it off when I picked up a sandwich from the deli. Are you sure you're feeling up to it?"

"Yes. I want to find out more about Miranda and Dr. Porter." She knew he was just as curious.

"Then how about we meet for dinner at Rigatoni's? I'll text you the time later."

"That is a wonderful idea. See you for dinner." She closed the connection and didn't have one bit of guilt over not telling him about visiting with Martha Samples.

~*~

Ryan stared at his phone. He had a niggling feeling Shandra was up to more than seeing Miranda, but he couldn't figure out what. He washed down the rest of the turkey sandwich he'd picked up from the deli, and opened up his laptop to the file on Dana Alvarez. The last entry on her criminal history was the theft of a diamond necklace from Mrs. Gladys Narvel.

This information led him to wonder if she had gone back to steal something else and had been caught by the older woman.

He closed his laptop and headed to the room where Dana was being held for his questioning.

Blane stood outside the door. "You know we picked her up for theft from Mrs. Narvel a few months ago."

"Yes, I do. That's one of the reasons I'm questioning her." He grasped the door handle.

"Do you think she killed the old lady?"

"That's what I'm going to find out." Ryan opened the door and stepped inside the small, drab room.

Dana glared at him, her arms crossed. She didn't act like anyone who was scared of going to jail for murder. After reading her sheet, he had a feeling she was tougher than her mother.

He opened his computer and scanned the information. Her father had gone to jail when she was small. If she wasn't careful she'd follow in his footsteps.

"Why did you go to Mrs. Narvel's house when you knew she didn't want you around?" He'd start with the easy questions.

"That's where my mom lives, and I needed money." Her knees under the table bounced. He could feel the vibration in the floor.

"Did your mom give you money?"

"No! She told me she couldn't help me anymore. She didn't want to lose her job with Mrs. Narvel." The young woman laughed. "Looks like she won't have a job much longer with that old bat gone."

He studied Dana. "Why do you say that? Dr. Porter will need a housekeeper."

Her arms unfolded and she leaned on the table. "That may be, but he may not be living in the house."

"Why wouldn't he? He's the heir." It appeared the thief knew quite a bit about the household.

"I heard that writer on the phone. He said he could get more money out of Dr. Porter than the old woman." She leaned back, a smug smile on her face. "He was blackmailing poor old aunty."

He had a suspicion the why was on the recordings. "Do you know what he was blackmailing her about?"

"Something that happened a long time ago."

"When did you hear this?" He wasn't sure if she'd made it up or was actually telling the truth.

"When I took the necklace. Mrs. Narvel and the doctor had gone out. I could hear the writer tapping away on his keyboard when I snuck up the stairs. I picked up the necklace and was in the hall getting ready to go downstairs when I heard his phone ring. He answered and was all happy saying how he'd get more money from the doctor. He cared more about property or something like that."

"Propriety?"

She snapped her fingers. "Yeah, that's the word."

Ryan had typed the notes into his computer. "What about yesterday? What were you doing at the house?"

"I'd talked mom into letting me stay with her. I told her, I'd go in and out the service door in the back and no one would know I was around." The young woman's attitude had lightened as she talked of her good fortune.

"Were you in the house when the murder happened?"

Her eyes grew larger. "Murder? What are you talking about? I thought she fell down the stairs."

He didn't think the surprise was fake. "Didn't your mom tell you Mrs. Narvel didn't fall down the stairs on her own?"

"N-no. I saw her, lying there at the bottom of the stairs and figured she tripped or fell or something." She nibbled on the side of her fingernail.

"You saw her in the hallway? Why didn't you call your mother?" He narrowed his eyes. "Or did you and that's why you left. Your mother didn't want anyone seeing you at the house. Does she think you pushed her employer?"

"No. She just told me to leave. To not be there when the police showed up because of my past." Dana shook her head. "I didn't push her down the stairs."

"Was anyone else in the house at the time?"

She dropped her hand into her lap. "Not that I know of. That writer left about eleven thirty. I heard him drive off when I was sitting in the kitchen eating."

Ryan had a gut feeling she was telling the truth,

but he'd have to get a statement from Holmes about when he left. It would also help to have the coroner's findings. "Sit tight. I'll get this information printed out and you can sign it."

"Does that mean I can leave?" The awe in her voice made him grin.

"You can go, but don't leave town. I may have more questions for you." He wasn't writing her off as the possible murderer, but she had given him more to go on.

~*~

Shandra sat in Lil's pickup outside the city recorder's office. They'd picked up her pills and she'd taken one with a bottle of water.

When she'd told Lil she was going to town, her employee had been adamant she shouldn't be driving. Lil had forced Shandra into the pickup and told her she'd run her around until she needed to be dropped off at the restaurant for dinner.

"You didn't have to bring me to town. That garden would have been ready for planting if you had stayed home." Shandra gathered her purse and her notepad with the questions she wanted to ask Martha.

"I'd of never been able to work knowing you were driving all over tarnation." Her white hair stuck out from under her cap as she stared at the building in front of them. "What are you doing here?"

"I want Martha to look up something for me."

"You sure you want her to know what you're up to?" Lil's white brows nearly touched above her nose as she scowled.

"I'm only asking about the Narvel business history. Nothing worth gossiping about there." She opened the door. "If you want to go get coffee somewhere, I can walk over to Miranda's from here. In fact, you could go home. It's not that far from Miranda's to the restaurant. Or she can give me a lift, and I can wait there for Ryan."

"I'll be here when you come out." Lil shut off the vehicle and opened the newspaper she'd purchased at the pharmacy.

Shandra sighed and slid out of the passenger side. She straightened the calf-length skirt she'd put on in hopes of making her look and feel better. Glancing at her newest pair of cowboy boots, her spirits lifted. She'd waited for this pair of turquoise boots to go on sale and was rewarded with capturing a pair.

She shoved open the doors and walked up to the counter.

Martha sat behind a desk ten feet beyond the counter. Her bleached-blonde head raised. Her eyes narrowed behind the glasses, sitting halfway down her nose. "What do you want?"

It appeared Martha still held some animosity toward Shandra for thinking she'd killed Johnny Clark.

"I'm here looking into who backed Mr. Narvel on building the ski resort." She wasn't going to let the woman's attitude keep her from digging into what she needed to know.

"Mr. Narvel? You think that has something to

do with Mrs. Narvel's death? I thought it was an accident?" Martha sprang out of the chair and leaned on the counter. "I would think you'd know if it was murder or an accident since you are living with a detective."

Shandra held back the "none of your business" remark she wanted to say and asked, "You do have the records for nineteen-seventy, don't you?"

"We have records clear back to when this town became incorporated." Martha poised a pen over a small pad of paper. "What do you want?"

"I would like to know who the men or businesses were who backed the building of the resort. From the papers, I noted backers were mentioned and I wanted to see who they were. For my own curiosity. That was a large venture for anyone to make on a small community at that time."

Martha disappeared into a back room and came back with a large book. "All the incorporation papers and land sales are in this book." She placed the book on a table in the small waiting area.

"Do you know where in the book?" Shandra sat down in front of the book and opened the cover.

"That is nineteen-seventy. The papers are in chronological order. That's the best I can tell you." Martha brushed her hands together as if the book had been dusty and walked back behind the counter.

Shandra sighed and flipped the pages, reading the documents.

Chapter Nine

Ryan walked into the small office Chief Sandberg at the Huckleberry Police gave him when he was working a case in the resort town. He opened his computer to send his report on his interview with Dana Alvarez to Sheriff Oldham when an e-mail dinged. Sheila Rickman, the state coroner in Coeur d'Alene.

He opened the document and started reading. Besides the bruising he'd noticed on the wrists, there was unexplained bruising and tearing of skin on her left shoulder. The fall had broken several bones and caused a hemorrhage in her brain. The cause of death was cited as complications of blunt trauma with chronic obstructive pulmonary disease also a significant condition contributing to death. Definite finger marks on her wrists. All bruising was new. Time of death was sometime between ten and noon. He stared at the screen. "The fall and lack of oxygen killed her. Whoever tossed her down the stairs knew without oxygen she'd die. We need to find the missing oxygen canister." He used a piece of paper and listed all the people in the house who knew about her need for oxygen and who were in the house before noon. This earlier time frame added Holmes to the list of suspects along with Mrs. Alvarez and Dana.

His phone rang.

"Detective Greer."

"Detective, this is Dalmar Jarvis, you left a message for me to call you." There was enough warble in the man's voice for Ryan to judge him to be in his sixties.

"Yes, Mr. Jarvis. Thank you for calling me back. Had you heard Mrs. Narvel died?"

"Yes, sad, sad news. She gave a lot to this community."

"I'm investigating her death—"

The lawyer's intake of breath stopped his comment. "It wasn't natural causes?"

"No. I just read the coroner's report and it was homicide."

"Who would want to do something like that to Mrs. Narvel?" The indignation in the man's voice made Ryan grin.

"That's what I'm trying to find out. What can you tell me about the will?"

"You don't think her nephew had anything to do with this? He adored his aunt. They came into the office a couple of times. We also handled the monies used for his research."

The conversation was headed where he wanted

it to go. "How was the money allotted to Dr. Porter for his research?"

"On an 'as needed' basis."

"He'd just walk in or call you up and say he needed more money?" It made him wonder if the doctor had been taking more than he was using.

"No. He'd come in with his aunt and hand me papers stating what he needed the money for or how he would use it. Always meticulous paperwork. If his aunt and I agreed, we'd put the amount in his research fund."

Dr. Porter was proving to be as business-minded with his aunt as with his research and profession. "What about the will. Does it name anyone other than Dr. Porter?"

Mr. Jarvis cleared his throat. "Well, yes, and no. The will states all of her belongings and monies go to her living heir or heirs."

"Why did she have heir or heirs?" Did she have an inkling someone from her adopted daughter would turn up?

"She had hoped to live long enough to see her nephew married and with children." He cleared his throat again. "I'm not one to discuss my clients, but since she's dead...Mrs. Narvel wanted desperately for her nephew to live past fifty. That's why she put him through college and paid for all his research. She wanted the Porter line to continue. She thought highly of her father and brother. She would go on and on some visits about how she wished there had been more female heirs because the males were predestined to die early."

If Mrs. Narvel hadn't been killed, she may have seen her wish come true if the interaction he'd witnessed between the doctor and Miranda last night was any indication of their relationship.

"Did she ever ask you to look for a relative?" He didn't want to give away the woman's secrets, even if she was dead.

"Years ago she asked me to look up a convent in the Midwest, but it had caught fire and the records were all gone." His voice trailed off. Shuffling papers sounded in the phone. "The Sisters of the Holy Cross in Omaha."

"Thank you. If you think of anything else, please call." Ryan pressed the off button and dialed the Sheriff's Department.

"Weippe County Sheriff's Department," Cathleen answered.

"This is Ryan. Has anyone had time to copy the manuscript on the laptop and the recording on the device I sent over with Trapp?"

"Ron printed the manuscript. He's still working on the recording."

"Have him bring it all back to me as soon as he gets the recording copied. I think there is information on one of those that will help my investigation."

"Will do. You'll be at Shandra's correct?" The singsong tone in her voice made him cringe.

"We're having dinner in Huckleberry tonight. Have Ron call me when he hits town. He may not have to go all the way out to the ranch." He pushed the off button before his sister made some crack about them going out to dinner. The more his sisters and mother pushed him to marry, the harder he pushed against it. He hadn't told the women in his life that he and Shandra had been easing their way toward mentioning the "m" word in their conversations. They were both still a bit head-shy after past experiences and having been on their own for so long.

He glanced at his watch. Four-thirty. It looked like they would have an early dinner tonight. All he had left to do was write up his conversation with the lawyer and add the coroner's report to his file.

~*~

Shandra walked out of the Recorder's Office with several corporation and individual's names. Lil sat in her pickup, waiting.

"You should have got what you wanted, you were in there long enough," the older woman groused as she turned the key and pulled out of the parking lot.

"I did. I told you, you didn't have to stay." But even as she said it, she was glad Lil had been her stubborn self. Even though all she'd done was sit and read, her head had started to pound and her energy was ebbing.

"Where does Miranda live?" Lil asked.

"The old apartment building on the edge of town across from the theatre and beside the Chalet Lodge motel." Shandra leaned her head back, closing her eyes.

"You sure you don't want me to take you home? You're losing color." Lil's voice wasn't as gruff as before.

"I'm fine." She opened the water bottle she'd used to take the prescribed pill and swallowed two pain relievers.

They drove down Huckleberry Street. Shandra glanced in the windows of Dimensions Gallery. Her friends, Ted and Naomi, owned the gallery and showcased her work. She could see the area in the middle with her vases where anyone walking by and into the building would see them.

Lil parked the vehicle in front of the apartments. "I'll wait here in case she isn't home."

Shandra pulled out her phone. "I'll call and check."

The phone rang three times before Miranda picked up. "Hello?"

"Hi. This is Shandra. Do you have time to visit?" She could tell from the sounds in the background her friend was already at work at the restaurant.

"I'm at work. But come on over. I'm just making sure things are ready. Momma and Poppa left me to run the restaurant while they visit my brother in Seattle." Miranda's voice as always sounded excited to have her visit.

"As long as you don't think I'll be in the way."

Miranda laughed. "I would be disappointed if you didn't come see me after last night."

"See you in five." Shandra pressed the off button. "She's at the restaurant. Would you please drop me off there and go home?"

Lil snorted, put the vehicle in gear, and drove

them around the block, parking in front of the restaurant door. "I'll turn the lights on and have the fireplace going when you come home."

"Thank you, Lil. I do appreciate all you do for me, Sheba, the horses, and even Ryan."

"I don't do nothin' for Ryan," she spat and stared forward.

Shandra chuckled, stepped out of the pickup, and walked up to the door.

The pickup roared to life and Lil sped down the street. She'd hit a nerve with her employee. Lil and Ryan were slowly reconciling to the other, but it still wasn't one hundred percent for either one.

The door was locked. The sign said they opened at four-thirty. She noted on her phone it was just after four. She rapped on the glass door.

Miranda hurried over, her six foot, curvy body floated along on three inch heels. The young woman towered over most men and she still wore the high-heeled shoes when she worked at her family's restaurant.

The door opened and Shandra was pulled into a hug.

"It's good to see you. When Ryan said you were sick and Alex said you needed rest and antibiotics, I wasn't sure you'd be by today." Miranda held her at arm's length. "You look terrible."

She laughed at her friend's honesty. "Thanks! Ryan is meeting me here for dinner later, so if you want to tuck me in a booth that's fine."

"I'd rather talk with you where the staff can't

hear." Miranda led her to a booth in the far corner, with a view of the ski slopes. "Let me tell the staff I'll be visiting with you." Her long legs carried her through the tables and booths and into the kitchen.

Shandra studied the mountain. The snow was melting, leaving half the slope under the ski lifts new grass green and farther up rocks and snow.

"Here you go." Miranda carried a tray. She placed a pot of hot water, a honey pot—Shandra had made for the restaurant, two cups with steaming water, and an assortment of teas on the table. "Thought I'd join you."

They both picked a tea and dunked the bags before Miranda picked up her cup, took a drink, and said, "I know you probably think I'm a horrible friend for not telling you about Alex and me."

Shandra set her cup down. "Alex? I thought you and Dr. Porter were dating?"

"We are." Miranda took another sip of her tea.

"But I thought his name was Maynard? That's what it says on the clinic sign." Shandra always called the man Dr. Porter because the name Maynard sounded like a name for an old person.

"Maynard is his first name and was his father's and grandfather's. His middle name is Alexander and he prefers to be called Alex by his friends." She wrinkled her nose. "Maynard is so old sounding."

Shandra laughed. "That's what I thought. And no, you don't have to tell me everything, but I'm a terrible friend for not picking up on the fact you had a male friend. I mean, I realized you seemed happier, which with your personality is hard to notice.”

"My open optimism is what caught Alex's attention." Miranda sipped her tea and smiled before her expression grew somber. "Last December when I'd fallen for that horrible man's flirting and nearly got you, Maxine, and myself killed, I had sworn off men and dating. But after we came back, Momma made me go see Dr. Porter. She wanted a doctor to tell her I wasn't hurt physically." She smiled. "It was during that visit that I realized he was shy and socially awkward." Her cheeks flushed a healthy rose. "And that he found me attractive."

"Any man would be crazy not to find you attractive," Shandra said, smiling at her friend.

"Most flirt until I stand up or they do and realize I'm taller than they are. That doesn't bother Alex. He likes me just the way I am. And I like him for all his social ineptness and his logical brain." She sipped her tea. "He says I give him even more of a reason to complete his research." Her smile slipped and she leaned across the table. "He has some genetic disease that if he doesn't find a cure will kill him by the time he's fifty. He only has thirteen more years."

"I heard about that. It doesn't bother you that he may not find the cure?" Shandra thought about her feelings for Ryan. If she knew he would die in twelve years, she'd be clinging to all hope to keep him alive and spending as much time with him as she could.

"It bothers me. But we decided to make as

much of the time together as we can. He's taking me to Italy this summer. He wants to learn about my family and see my joy." She smiled. "He is so attentive and loving." Her gaze turned stormy. "And pigheaded. I couldn't believe he didn't tell me as soon as he knew his aunt had died. He loved her like a mother."

Shandra added more hot water to her cup. "Why didn't he tell you?"

"He received the call from Officer Blane when we were finishing up lunch. He said something was wrong at the house. That was it, 'something wrong at the house.' Then I didn't hear from him, so I called and he said he was headed to your place and his aunt was dead." She stared into her cup. "We've become so close, I don't understand why he didn't tell me right away. He said he was being questioned and trying to wrap his mind around this woman that claims to be his aunt's granddaughter and things the writer had said. His logical brain was trying to put everything in boxes and when things don't fit like he thinks they should, he goes abstract professor. Forgetful and not really listening, because his brain is working on the problem."

"This is interesting. I thought Dr. Porter was just one of those people who kept to himself, but you've told me so much that I feel for him even more than I did before." Shandra put a hand on Miranda's. "I'm glad he has you."

Dream a Little Dream played. She fished her phone out of her purse and smiled. "My dinner date."

"Hello."

"Hi Shandra, I've finished early are you ready for dinner?" Ryan asked.

"I'm at the restaurant already. Miranda's parents are gone and she had to be here early."

"Good. I'll be there in five."

The line went dead. "He's on his way."

"I'll clear away my things and get you two menus." Miranda stood. "It's good to have someone to talk to. We've been keeping our dating a secret. I don't know what Momma and Poppa will think. Alex is thirteen years older. It's not like he's after the restaurant and Momma knew his family before moving here. I just don't want them to be upset."

"I think you should tell them when they get back. I have a feeling they would be delighted to know you've found a man who can support you and who loves you." Shandra thought about Miranda mentioning her mother had known the family. "Which side of Dr. Porter's family did your mom know?"

"His father's side. She knew Mrs. Narvel before she married. The Narvel's asked Momma and Poppa to start this restaurant."

Rapping on the front door drew their attention. Ryan stood at the door waiting.

"It's four-thirty. Time to open." Miranda carried the tray with her cup to the door and let Ryan in.

He hurried to the booth, sliding in across from Shandra.

Chapter Ten

Ryan studied Shandra. Her complexion was pale, but her eyes were brighter than they'd been the last few days. "How are you feeling?"

"Tired, but better than I have been in days. Are you any closer to knowing who killed Mrs. Narvel?"

He shook his head. "No and you're not supposed to be interested in the case."

She smiled and pulled a small notebook out of her leather fringed purse. "Sorry, but I've grown even more interested since my conversation with Miranda."

"Why is that?"

"Did you know Dr. Porter likes to be called Alex? It's his middle name."

Caught off guard by her statement, he stared into her golden eyes. "What?"

"Miranda calls Dr. Porter, Alex, because it's his middle name and he likes his friends to call him that."

"What has this got to do with the investigation?" He picked up a glass of water a young server delivered to them.

"Nothing. It's one of the things I learned while talking with Miranda. Also, her mother knew Mrs. Narvel before they moved here and the Narvel's asked the Aducci's to start a restaurant here."

He smiled. "I know that and had hoped to talk with Mrs. Aducci while I was here."

"You won't be able to. Mr. and Mrs. Aducci are in Seattle visiting Miranda's brother."

"You told me that when I called." He placed his hand on her forehead to see if she was feverish. It would explain her repeating herself.

"Oh, that's right, I did. Sorry." She flipped open the notebook. "Before I came here, Lil took me to the city recorder's office."

He tapped her book with a finger. "Why would you do that?"

"To find out who the other backers were that helped Mr. Narvel build the ski resort." She sipped her tea.

The waitress arrived to take their orders. Ryan went with his usual fettucine and Shandra picked the minestrone soup. When the woman moved on, he pulled her notebook over in front of him.

Three names were printed on the page. Two he didn't know. The third had been linked to drug related cases. "These were the men who partnered with Mr. Narvel?"

She nodded. "I can tell you've heard of at least one of them."

He nodded. "Not someone a law-abiding citizen would associate with."

"Do you think Mrs. Narvel knew that? Do you think word of her memoirs somehow came to the man's attention?"

"I'm not even sure the elder Vince Barsotti is still alive. But his son, Vince, has his hands in all kinds of illegal schemes." Ryan pushed Shandra's notebook back in front of her. "The ski resort was running in nineteen-seventy that's forty-three years ago. Vince would have been a baby. I doubt he's worrying about any dirt on his father."

"Does that mean you aren't going to look into it?" Shandra closed the book and put it in her purse.

Miranda arrived with their dinners. "Here you go." She turned to Ryan. "Alex is coming here for dinner at six if you have any news you want to share with him." She watched Ryan as if he could say anything about the case to her or the doctor. Talking about it with Shandra was something he'd gotten used to, knowing she usually had some spiritual guidance.

"How's he holding up?" Ryan asked, avoiding the spilling of any information.

"He still can't believe it." Her voice stalled as her gaze roamed over to the door.

Ryan followed her narrowed gaze and discovered Mr. Holmes and Miss Tapfer looking cozy as they stood waiting for a seat. He put a hand on Miranda's arm. "Do me a favor and place them in the booth behind me."

She studied him a minute before her lips tipped into a grin. "Okay."

As she sauntered to the front door, he motioned for Shandra to sit by him. He pulled all of the dishes to the end nearest the window.

"Are we going to eavesdrop?" Shandra whispered in his ear.

"Something like that." He didn't mind having her sitting close. They rarely cozied up when out in the public. They both had a reputation to watch even though most of the town of Huckleberry knew the county detective spent most of his time at the pottery artists ranch on the mountain.

"Here you go. Notice the lovely view of the ski lift. In the winter at night this view is spectacular." Miranda's voice was as bubbly as always.

He heard people sliding into the booth behind them.

"Enjoy!" Miranda said and walked away.

"Thank you for bringing me here, Jeffery. I'm not sure what to do with myself now that Mrs. Narvel is dead."

Miss Tapfer's statement had him pressing against the back rest. Shandra had her eyes closed. It was her way of absorbing everything around her.

"It's my pleasure. We both just need to stay here until things are settled. I have to talk the nephew into letting me continue with the book and you need to establish your claim to half the money."

Mr. Holmes sounded confident that Miss

Tapfer would get the money. Did he have proof other than the reminisces of an old woman?

"I don't know if the birth certificate will be enough. Dr. Porter was stunned to learn about me. I have a feeling he may fight harder than you think."

A waitress arrived to get their drinks.

Ryan held his breath she didn't ask them how things were. She left as soon as the two behind them had ordered. He let out his breath. Miranda must have said something to her.

"From what I've learned from the old lady, Dr. Porter only has about twelve years left. He won't want to spend that time fighting you in the courts."

"What are you talking about?"

The man went on about the doctor's condition.

"Poor man." Miss Tapfer said. "Oh my! What about me? If we're the same family, should I be worried?"

"No, it only happens to male heirs. You're safe, baby."

The endearment sent Ryan's senses on alert. The woman sounded genuine, but the man sounded like a scam artist. He needed more background on him soon.

His phone buzzed. Glancing at the screen, it was Trapp. Damn! He needed to take the call, but didn't want the two to know he was here.

Shandra saw the war on Ryan's face. He needed to take the call but didn't want to be found. The couple didn't know her.

She grabbed Ryan's phone and darted out of the booth and into the waiting area.

"Shandra," she answered.

"What are you doing answering Ryan's phone?" the voice of a deputy she knew asked.

"He's detained listening in on a conversation between suspects." It was pretty much what he was doing and she didn't think it was illegal, everyone did it.

"I see. I have the manuscript and recording he wanted. I take it you're not at your place."

"No, we're at Rigatoni's. Are you in town?"

"Yes. I can be there in five."

"Come on in, I'll have Miranda put you in a booth, and I'll buy your dinner. Ryan will come to you." This sounded like a spy mission. She giggled.

"What's so funny," the man on the other end asked.

"Nothing." She hung up the phone and caught Miranda's gaze. Her friend walked over.

"Are you learning anything?" she asked.

"I'm not sure. A county deputy will be showing up any minute. Can you put him where the writer and woman can't see him? He has files for Ryan. And I'm buying his dinner." Shandra glanced toward the booths. Miss Tapfer was the one facing the doors. She didn't think a police officer coming in and being seated would rile her.

She wandered back to the booth and sat. A glance at the writer proved he didn't care that she had been sitting in the booth. She slid in next to Ryan and handed him his phone. Leaning close she whispered in his ear, "I'm buying Deputy Trapp's dinner. Miranda will seat him on the other side."

Ryan nodded.

"Have they said anything else interesting?" she whispered.

He shook his head and put a bite of food in his mouth.

She leaned forward and started eating her soup.

The couple must have been eating because they were quiet.

"Alex, no!" Miranda's voice carried across the room.

"What are you doing here?"

Dr. Porter's angry voice drew Shandra to the edge of the seat. She knew the minute he spotted the writer.

"And you! This confirms my belief you are a fake and you are a conspirator!"

Shandra slid out of the booth. "Dr. Porter, this isn't the time or place. Come on." She led the man away from the booth and over to where Miranda stood, her arms crossed and tapping one foot.

"That was a stupid thing to do," Miranda said to the doctor in a low hiss.

"It frustrates me to see the two of them together, knowing the lies they are trying to spread about Aunt Gladys." He put a hand on Miranda's arm. "Forgive me. I haven't been myself since yesterday."

Shandra eased away from the two. They had things to work out, besides his lack of tact. Walking back to the booth, she passed Miss Tapfer and the writer. The man was smiling and the woman looked upset.

She plopped down on the bench beside Ryan. "The two you were spying on are leaving and Dr. Porter is being consoled by Miranda."

Ryan bumped her hip with his. "Let's get the items from Trapp and get home. It's going to be a long night reading and listening."

Chapter Eleven

Shandra hadn't met Mrs. Narvel but listening to the woman tell her story, she felt as if they had been friends. The woman's love of life was evident in the escapades of her childhood and young adult life. Her voice became vehement and angry when she told of the man who stole her innocence and the anger she harbored toward her family for not believing how she'd become pregnant. Her time in the convent was a jail sentence to her. She hadn't even looked at her child before it was whisked away to a waiting couple. "I didn't want to see the man who defiled me in the child's face."

She could understand the young woman's torment. But still it had been her flesh and blood. Surely somewhere in her lifetime she'd wanted to see the child? Find out if it was doing well.

Ryan nodded off when Mrs. Narvel was telling

about her college dating.

Shandra nudged his arm. "Let's go to bed. This will be here in the morning."

"Yeah, I won't be able to hear anything if I'm snoring." He rose and headed to the kitchen with the empty wine glasses and the dessert boxes. Miranda had sent them home with dessert. She said it was her thank you for Shandra stepping in and pulling Alex away from causing a scene.

Shandra went to the front door and called Sheba in. The clumsy dog ran into the house, sliding the rug in front of the door into the hallway.

"I'll get that," Ryan said, walking out of the kitchen.

"Thanks. I'm doing better but bending over starts my head throbbing." She headed to bed. Within minutes of lying down, she was asleep and dreaming.

Ella held a baby as she sat on a gravestone. "Who is this?" Shandra asked, striding through the graveyard toward her grandmother. The white wisps of cloud moved and she saw a name. May Alexandra Porter. "What are you saying? A girl was born but didn't live? Then Miss Tapfer is a fake."

Shandra woke, her mind still seeing the name on the gravestone. She ran a hand over her face. The name was so close to Dr. Porter's, was that a coincidence or something else?

She sat up and grabbed her robe from the end of the bed. Sleep wasn't going to come. Sheba followed her out into the main room. She made a cup of hot chocolate, rewound the recording to the time when Mrs. Narvel was sent to the convent, and listened again.

~*~

Ryan woke and felt a cold draft coming from Shandra's side of the bed. He reached over and found cold sheets. Swinging his legs over the side of the bed, he slid his feet into slippers and headed to the main room.

Sheba slept in front of the dead fireplace. Shandra was asleep on the couch. The recording was still playing. Mrs. Narvel was talking about her wedding to Mr. Narvel. She sounded like a woman getting ready to set forth on a magical journey. He turned the device off, draped a blanket over Shandra, and went back to bed. He'd have to ask Shandra why she was back listening to the recording in the morning. She needed her sleep.

He returned to bed but didn't fall asleep until he'd run all the information they had so far over in his mind.

~*~

Shandra woke with a stiff neck, but her head was clearer than it had been for a week. She stared at the fireplace and then down at the blanket on her. The dream and coming out to listen to the recording came back to her.

Clanging in the kitchen meant Ryan was up and fixing breakfast. She stretched and headed in for a cup of coffee. The scents of bacon, coffee, and her cinnamon rolls filled the air, making her stomach growl.

"You're going all out with breakfast. You hungry or wanting to celebrate a breakthrough?"

Ryan turned from the stove and grinned. "I was hungry. For some reason, I love the food at Rigatoni's but I'm always starving in the morning after eating it."

"Too many carbs." She slid onto a stool and watched him cook. It was moments like this that she found herself imagining spending the rest of her life with him. A smile crept onto her lips. He'd be surprised if she proposed to him.

He placed a plate on the counter in front of her and grinned. "That's a smile full of mischief, what are you thinking?" He leaned forward, placing his elbows on the counter, and his face only a foot from hers.

Her heart stuttered. But her mind stopped the words from blurting out. "You'll just have to wait and see." She cut into the cinnamon roll and savored the burst of spice, sweetness, and yeasty goodness.

Ryan straightened and picked up another plate, sitting on the stool next to her. "What were you doing back up listening to the recording?"

She sipped the coffee and faced him. "I had a dream. Ella was holding a baby and sitting on a gravestone. The name on the stone was May Alexandra Porter." She studied his expression but he gave away nothing. "I think Mrs. Narvel's baby died and was never given up for adoption. Which would make Miss Tapfer's claims false."

"What makes you think that?"

"The name on the gravestone. If the baby was a girl and had been given up for adoption, the parents would have named her something other than the family names of the Porters."

He nodded. "That makes sense. We need to see if there is anyone left who was at the convent and remembers the birth. And we need to see the birth certificate Miss Tapfer was waving around."

Shandra continued to eat. "If her baby died, why don't you think she mentioned it in her memoirs?"

"Maybe she didn't know?" Ryan raised a forkful of food toward his mouth.

"But the name on the stone had to have come from her or her family." She picked up her coffee and faced him. "And why is it so close to Dr. Porter's name? How would her brother have come up with a name for his child that is so close to the one his sister lost?" She shook her head. "Someone in the family had to know about the baby."

"All we have is your dream to think the baby died. That's circumstantial evidence. Nothing we can say to anyone. I'm going to concentrate on the authenticity of the birth certificate and get someone checking into the records at the convent." He'd finished his food. Ryan stood and placed his dishes in the sink. "I'm going to make a few calls then finish listening to that recording."

Shandra nodded. She wanted to hear the rest of the recordings as well. Moving slow to keep her head from pounding, she cleaned up the kitchen and returned to the main room as Ryan finished his phone call.

She placed a tray with two cups of coffee on the table by the couch and settled down, pulling a blanket around her.

Ryan started the recording where they'd left off the night before.

An hour and a half later, she sat up. "Did you hear that?"

"What?" Ryan stopped the recording device. "What did you hear?"

"A click, like something had been erased." She leaned forward, taking the device from him and rewinding. "Listen." She clicked the play button.

"My husband was an astute man. He knew bringing 'click' these men had money."

She stopped it. "Not only is there the faint click but the sentence doesn't make sense. This has been edited."

"I'll call Ron and see if he was interrupted and could have lost the words." Ryan pulled out his phone.

"Where's the manuscript? I'll see if there is any mention of the men in it." Shandra held out her hands.

Ryan dropped the thick manila envelope the deputy brought Ryan last night into her lap.

She opened the flap and flipped through the pages until she reached the time in Mrs. Narvel's life when the ski resort was becoming a reality. She found the names of two of the men she'd dug up, but not the third. The one that Ryan knew the history on.

Ryan finished his conversation. "Ron said he didn't have any interruptions. The good thing is we still have the original recording. He's taking it to the State Police lab to see if there is any way to retrieve whatever was recorded over." He sat down next to her. "Did you find anything?"

"The book names two of the men who helped fund the ski resort."

"Let me guess, not Vince Barsotti."

She nodded. "Why leave him out? Was the money he lent Mr. Narvel tainted? Did the Narvels know about it?" She studied Ryan.

"Or that's who Mr. Holmes is blackmailing. There's one way to find out. I'll call my contacts in Seattle and see what they can find out about dealings between Mr. Narvel and Mr. Barsotti." Ryan rose off the couch and walked into the kitchen.

Shandra pulled her laptop onto her lap and typed in convents in Omaha, Nebraska. She wanted to find out if there was a baby in a cemetery there with the name May Alexandra Porter.

Chapter Twelve

Ryan sped along the county road. He'd left Shandra scanning the internet for cemeteries while he went to question Mr. Holmes and Miss Tapfer. He'd called ahead and asked Chief Sandberg to have one of his men bring the two into the Huckleberry Police Station.

At the edge of town, he slowed and made a circuit of the Chalet Lodge Motel, Miranda's apartment building, and the Narvel Victorian house outside of town, before heading to the police station. As he turned the corner to park at the station, he noticed Dr. Porter's car in the clinic parking lot. It appeared he believed work would help him through his grief better than Miranda.

Ryan stepped through the door and heard Mr. Holmes arguing with someone.

"Your two are here," Hazel said, nodding

toward the rooms in the back.

"They were put in separate rooms, I hope." The small police force was pretty efficient, but they did tend to blunder a bit when dealing with more than one suspect at a time.

"Yes. The man didn't like how Blane brought him in." Hazel's eyes sparkled with merriment.

"I see. Did Mr. Holmes have handcuffs?"

She grinned and bobbed her gray curls. "He did."

Ryan shook his head. "I'll let him cool down and talk to Miss Tapfer first." He carried his laptop under his arm as he entered the quiet interview room.

Miss Tapfer was staring at the door. Her eyes were wide and her hands clenched together on top of the table. He assumed the purse next to her arm was hers.

"Miss Tapfer, you can relax. I just have a few questions for you." Ryan sat down across the table from her and opened his laptop. He had the files Cathleen had put together on the woman and the writer on his screen.

"That police officer hauled me in here liked I'd committed a crime. And I thought I heard Jeffrey's voice a few minutes ago." Her hands remained clenched, her posture alert.

"That was Mr. Holmes you heard. I'll be speaking with him next." Ryan scanned the information. "Where do you live?"

"Sun City, California." She studied him. "Why?"

"Did you know Mr. Holmes before coming here?"

"Yes. When he came looking for my mother after her death." She narrowed her eyes. "Do you think we made this all up?"

"I'm trying to understand why you would show up the day Mrs. Narvel is murdered and insist you are her granddaughter. Especially, since you know Mr. Holmes so well. The only person, up until you arrived, who knew the woman had had a child."

"I'm telling you the truth." She reached into the purse and pulled out and off-white card, slapping the paper on the table in front of him. "Take a look at my grandmother's name."

Ryan scanned the document. It was well-worn, heavy stock paper that had a soft feel. The inserted information had been done with an older typewriter. Some words rose above the lines and others a bit under. The ink of the type was faded. He focused on the typed words, stopping at the child's name, May Alexandra Porter and then the mother's name, Gladys May Porter. No father's name. He rubbed his forehead. If this woman's mother was the baby, then what had Shandra seen in her dream?

"Do you mind if I keep this for a short time?" He had to admit it looked official, but he'd have someone else take a look at it.

"As long as I get it back. It's my only proof I'm Gladys Narvel's granddaughter." She settled back in the chair.

"Did Mr. Holmes come to you before you found the birth certificate?" He had to find out how, if the birth certificate was forged, it had come into her possession.

"Yes. It was his finding me and telling me my grandmother's story that sent me looking for the boxes I'd stored." She picked at her purse. "At first, I thought his story was some scam. But I looked up Mrs. Narvel online, reading the old newspaper articles and thought maybe what Jeffery had said could be true. That's when I found the box with the birth certificate and asked my grandmother about the names."

He reread his notes from the day of the murder. They had both left out the meeting before she found the birth certificate. It had sounded like Holmes quit looking after finding the mother was deceased. And that Miss Tapfer had discovered the birth certificate without any nudging. Different from this story. He wondered what the story would be tomorrow.

"I see. You didn't look for the birth certificate until Mr. Holmes had approached you about possibly being the granddaughter of a rich woman?"

She frowned. "That makes me sound like a gold-digger."

He shrugged. "From where Dr. Porter stands, that's what you look like."

"Well, I'm not. If he could get to know me, he'd see, I only want to learn more about a side of the family I didn't know."

"You could do that without brandishing the birth certificate like a membership card."

"I don't think I want to talk to you anymore." She crossed her arms and sat back in the chair, her lips pressed tight.

He sighed. At least he had the document. He left the room and carried the certificate up to the front. "Hazel, please bag this and have someone get it to the State lab ASAP. I want to know if it is legit." He pivoted to head back down the hall and stopped at Blane's desk. "I had a complaint about how you picked up Miss Tapfer. How about you go let her know she is free to go and politely take her back to her motel."

The young officer scowled but nodded his head.

"You'll get more out of suspects by being nice than by treating them as criminals before the fact." He strode down the hall to the room where Mr. Jeffrey Holmes, author and ghost writer, sat fuming.

The minute the door opened, the man said, "It's about time someone told me why I was dragged down here in handcuffs."

Ryan stepped in the room and noted the man still wore cuffs. He sighed. Chief Sandberg really needed to do something about Blane.

"Let me get those off. I'm afraid the youngest member of the Huckleberry P.D. thinks he has to be the bad cop all the time." Ryan pulled out his cuff key and released the writer from his metal bracelets.

"Thank you." Holmes rubbed his wrists and sat down. "Any chance I can get something to drink. My throat's dry."

From all the yelling he'd heard when he walked in the station. "Sure." Ryan stuck his head out the door. "Hazel, would you please bring Mr.

Holmes some water." He sat down across from the man and opened his computer. "Do you mind if I take notes?"

"Go ahead. It will be interesting to see how a cop works. Might have one in my next book." Holmes' face lit up, and he leaned back in his chair, completely at ease now that the handcuffs had been removed.

A soft knock on the door, and Hazel entered with a bottle of water.

"Thank you," Ryan said, handing the bottle to Holmes.

She nodded and backed out of the room.

The man guzzled all the water and wiped his mouth with his hand. "Thanks."

Ryan nodded. "When did you say you first learned about Mrs. Narvel's baby?"

"I thought I was dragged in here because I was a suspect." Holmes leaned forward, placing his forearms on the table.

"No. I'm trying to establish who might have helped Mrs. Narvel to an early end." He studied the man. "When did you learn about the baby? What did she say exactly?"

"You should know, you took the tapes and what I had written so far." Holmes leaned back in his chair.

"I haven't had time to go through them." A bit of a fabrication. He hadn't heard or read it all.

"I discovered in December, I think. Yes. She made a comment that she'd never sent a gift to her child. I asked her what child since no one had ever mentioned a son or daughter." He rattled off what had been said on the tape.

"And you decided to try and find her daughter out of the goodness of your heart?" Ryan didn't look up.

"Well, yeah. I though with some of my connections I might be able to tell her what had happened. I sent a P.I. I know to the convent. He gathered the records and sent them to me. That's how I found Mrs. Tapfer and discovered she was dead."

Ryan knew the convent had burned and all the records with it. The man was lying. "And when you found she was gone you stopped looking any further?"

"Yeah."

"Then how do you explain that you knew Miss Tapfer before you told her she could be the granddaughter of a rich woman?"

Holmes slammed his hands on the table and half stood. "Who said I knew her before I discovered she was the granddaughter?"

"She did."

Shandra couldn't believe her good fortune. She'd found a curator of the convent cemetery that knew the exact gravestone she was looking for. He'd promised to take a photo and send it to her phone.

She didn't want to work or stay at home. She'd go to Huckleberry, visit Ruthie and Naomi and hope the curator came through with the photo, then she could show Ryan. It would put a stop to Mr. Holmes and Miss Tapfer's claims she was Mrs. Narvel's granddaughter.

"Where're you goin'?" Lil asked when Shandra entered the barn to get her Jeep.

"To town."

"What about those things you need to put together for the show this month?"

Her employee was right. She needed to be thinking more about the upcoming show and less about Mrs. Narvel.

"You're right. I'll go work in the studio." She retraced her steps to the studio and walked inside. Three vases of varying sizes sat on the cooling table. They were ready to go other than needing to be packed. What she needed to put together were the supplies and instruments she'd need for the demonstration she was signed up to give.

Puttering around in the studio, the afternoon passed quickly. She was about to give up on the curator when her phone buzzed. A glance at the screen had her heart racing. The curator.

She swiped the screen and a photo of a gravestone looking exactly like the one in her dream appeared in color. Etched in the stone was the name, May Alexandra Porter. Born 8/3/1953 Died 8/5/1953. The child had only lived two days. Had Mrs. Narvel known that or had she gone to her death believing she had a daughter still alive?

Shandra saved the photo before forwarding it to Ryan. *This is what the curator at the cemetery sent me.*

Within minutes, *Dream a Little Dream* tinkled from her phone.

She answered and Ryan didn't even wait for her to say hello.

"This proves the two have been lying. I caught them both up in several lies today while questioning them. Once I get the findings on the birth certificate, we'll have even more to catch them up. Good job."

"Thank you. Will you be home for dinner?"

"No. I'll be getting in late. I have to finish up the paperwork and wait for the lab to get back to me about the certificate and the glitch in the recording."

"Ok. Do you mind if I continue to listen to the recording?" She didn't know if there would be any more evidence, she however, had become even more interested in the late Mrs. Narvel's life.

"Go ahead. Write down anything you think might be of importance."

"I will. Bye."

She shoved her phone in her pocket, tidied up the studio, and headed to the house. Ryan's allowing her to hear the recordings and helping with the investigation proved he trusted her. And she had to admit, she'd trusted him with her life on more than one occasion.

Sheba ran out of the trees behind the house. She had snowballs hanging on the hair above her paws.

"You must have found a snow pile that hasn't melted yet. Come on. I'll de-snow you." She let the dog into the house and the laundry room. Sheba stepped into the small shower stall used mainly for cleaning her up. Shandra used a comb to pull the snow from the dog's fur.

"There you go." Shandra stood as her phone jingled.

"Hello?"

"It's Miranda. I was wondering if you and Ryan would like to have dinner with Alex and I tomorrow night at his house?" Miranda's unsure voice caught Shandra's attention.

"I'll have to see if Ryan is free. Why are you having us over? Not that it's a big thing but I would have thought you'd invite us to your apartment."

Miranda blew out a breath. "That's what I wanted to do, but Alex said he wanted to use his aunt's house. He's invited my parents. I think he wants to show them he can provide for me if we, you know."

"Oh! Has he asked you to marry him?" Shandra was happy and sad for her friend, knowing that if the doctor didn't come up with a cure, Miranda could be a widow in twelve to thirteen years.

"No, not outright. I think he might tomorrow night. I think that's why he wants my parents there. And he said I could invite you since you're the closest friend I have lately. And well if we invite you, we have to invite Ryan so it's an even number." Her words wobbled a bit.

"Will you say yes if he asks you?" She didn't want her friend entering into marriage just because she felt sorry for the man.

"Yes. I know if he doesn't find a cure, I'll be a

young widow, but how can I pass up the years until then? I do love him, even if we seem an unusual couple." She sighed. "And Momma did know his family so it's not like I'm marrying into a serial killing family." She laughed.

Shandra wanted to laugh but she knew of the connection between Mr. Narvel and Vince Barsotti. "That's true," she offered. "I'll let you know about Ryan in the morning but you can count on me being there to celebrate with you."

"Thanks. I have to go. The restaurant is getting busy. It is Saturday night."

The connection went silent.

Saturday night. She hadn't even thought about what day it was. That happened a lot when Ryan was working a case and she was engrossed in a new project.

She poured a glass of wine, added sliced cheese to a plate with crackers, and settled on the couch to listen to more of the recording. Her mind circled back to the fact they would be having dinner in the Narvel house, where a murder had occurred only four days earlier. A sense of dread landed in her stomach.

Chapter Thirteen

Ryan still had Holmes in the interview room. They'd been at it for a couple of hours. The man had side-stepped and renounced some of his earlier statements, after hearing what Miss Tapfer said about them being friends before he'd come to her with the information.

He sent the photo from Shandra to his computer and then re-entered the room.

"When are you going to let me go? You say I'm not a suspect but you've been grillin' me like I am." Holmes stood behind the chair he'd been sitting in.

"I happen to have received a photograph from a curator at an Omaha cemetery. One that was part of the Sisters of the Holy Cross Convent."

The man's face paled. He pulled the chair out and plopped into it.

"I have a feeling you know what I'm going to show you." Ryan brought the photo up on his screen and spun it to face the man.

Holmes' gaze locked onto the screen. He heaved a heavy sigh and deflated against the chair back. "I didn't think to look in a cemetery."

"When you discovered all the records were gone, you decided to try and pawn Miss Tapfer, a woman who had lost her mother and had no one to tell her you were using her for a scam, off as Mrs. Narvel's granddaughter."

The writer didn't say anything.

"From Miss Tapfer's answers, she believes every word you told her and what I'm pretty sure we'll find to be a fake birth certificate. How did you find someone who was adopted with the name May Alexandra? And who had passed away? That was what sucked Miss Tapfer in. And would have worked on anyone, except Mrs. Narvel. She knew her daughter had died."

"I want a lawyer." Holmes crossed his arms and glared at him. He'd realized his game was up.

"I'm thinking when Miss Tapfer called Mrs. Narvel and said she was her granddaughter the woman knew you had to have been the one to put her up to pretending she was May's daughter. Mrs. Narvel must have waited until the next morning to confront you."

The man shot forward in his chair. "That was it. She didn't confront me. She asked me to bring Miss

Tapfer to her. She said to bring her in the afternoon so they could talk. I thought it was going to work. She was so family crazy, I thought she'd be willing to take in anyone as a member."

Ryan studied the man. He appeared to be perplexed over the woman asking him to bring Miss Tapfer.

~*~

Ryan pulled up to Shandra's log house and flicked the key off. The lights were all on. Either she fell asleep waiting for him or she was still listening to the recording. He grabbed his laptop and the tiramisu he'd purchased at Rigatoni's for Shandra. Finding the gravestone in the cemetery and the labs assessment that the birth certificate had been altered, were the clues needed to prove the granddaughter scam. He'd question Holmes tomorrow. Now he had to prove the man killed Mrs. Narvel to keep the scam alive.

Sheba was whimpering at the door.

His heart started racing and his senses kicked in. Why wasn't the dog happy to see him instead of sounding scared or sad. He pulled out his revolver, put his hand on the door knob, and slowly opened the door.

He scanned what he could see from the partially open door. Shandra lay on the couch, crying. Sheba sat beside the couch, whimpering and nuzzling her master.

Ryan crossed the room at a jog. "What's wrong?" He scooped Shandra up in his arms, assessing her for injuries.

Her eyes slowly fluttered open. She wrapped her arms around his neck and clung to him as if he were a tree and she feared a strong wind would pull her away.

"Shhh. I'm here. What were you dreaming?" He held her close, feeling her deep breaths, hearing her sniffles as she regained control.

She released his neck and leaned back, peering into his eyes. "I listened to more of the recording. There is a part where she is arguing with a Dana. The young woman apparently stole a necklace."

"Yes. Charges were brought against her and she was convicted. She is the woman you saw the day of the murder." He settled on the couch and settled Shandra on his lap. "Were there threats made?"

"Yes, by Mrs. Narvel. She said if Dana didn't stay out of her house, she'd get a restraining order. The woman said, then how was she to see her mother? Mrs. Narvel replied, she could be fired." Shandra peered into his eyes. "Do you think Dana would kill the older woman so her mother could keep her job?"

"She's a bitter young woman. From what I could tell, if her mother losing her job kept her from what she found easy pickings, stealing jewelry and such, I could see her shoving the old woman down the stairs." He didn't like to think of someone so young being that cold-hearted, but she had revealed signs of violence. "Is that what had you crying in your sleep?"

"No. Ella was in my dream. So was Mrs.

Narvel. She was crying over the baby. It doesn't make sense, but I felt her loss. Then Dr. Porter walked into my dream. He had his arms out as if waiting for someone to run into them. But no one came." She grabbed his forearm in a death grip. "Miranda called tonight. She wants us to join her, Dr. Porter, and her parents at Mrs. Narvel's for dinner tomorrow night. She thinks he's going to ask her father for her hand and then propose. She told me tonight, she would say yes, but the dream had the doctor empty-handed. Do you think her parents will object?"

Ryan rubbed soothing circles on her back. "I think because of the death in that house, the doctor's genetic short future, and the age difference, her parents could possibly object." He shifted to cop mode. "If her parents will be there, that means they will be back from Seattle." Should he talk with Mrs. Aducci in the morning or at the dinner?

"I think they are back already." Shandra shifted, sliding off his lap and onto the couch beside him. "The dream just made me feel empty and sad."

He tipped her face up to look into his. "You will never be alone as long as I have a breath of life in me."

She sniffed and smiled. "Ditto."

He kissed her until Sheba shoved her slobbery muzzle between them.

"I think someone wants to make sure you are okay." Ryan released Shandra and stood. "I picked up tiramisu from Rigatoni's, you want some?"

"Please." Shandra watched Ryan disappear into

the kitchen and hugged Sheba. "I have the two of you, don't I."

"Woof!"

She laughed and stood. "Yes, you may go outside." She still hadn't completely shaken off the sadness of the dream. Deep down she understood she was supposed to get something out of it other than loneliness. But what it was, she didn't know yet.

Walking back from letting Sheba out the front door, her gaze landed on the recording device. She'd noted the time on the recording and rewound it to the argument between Mrs. Narvel and the woman, Dana.

Ryan returned with two plates of tiramisu. He'd gone out of his way to bring her something she loved. All the little things he did that showed he cared should have left her with no doubts about their relationship. But her unhappy parents, then her stepfather bossing her mother around, and then her last relationship, years before Ryan came along, had all scared her of making any kind of legal commitment to anyone. Even someone as wonderful as Ryan.

He sat down next to her and pointed to the recording device sitting on the edge of the table. "Was Dana caught snooping around while Holmes was recording a session?"

She raised a heaped spoon to her mouth. "No. I think he heard the argument and taped it."

"Really? And he didn't mention this argument to me when he realized the death was a homicide?"

She nodded, savoring the rich caramel with the vanilla bean ice cream.

Ryan reached out, pressing the 'on' button. They listened to the argument.

This time she picked up on another sound and sat up, pointing at the device with her spoon. "Did you hear that?"

He stopped the recording and rewound, playing it again.

"There!" She exclaimed as the sound became even clearer.

"Someone else was listening besides Holmes. That was definitely a door closing beyond the two arguing." Ryan sat up. "I wonder if there is a page that corresponds to what they were talking about before he recorded the argument?" He grabbed up the pages of the manuscript.

"This is getting close to the end of the recording. Try the last two chapters of the memoir," Shandra suggested. She had yet to finish reading the manuscript. She'd found it easier to concentrate on the recording than the pages. Mrs. Narvel's voice and inflections made the story more interesting than the printed word.

"Here it is. I wonder if the lab techs can determine when this was written by checking the history on the computer?" He had his phone half way to his ear as he talked.

"What good will knowing when it was said do?" she asked, scooping another spoon of ice cream.

"I can question people about the day, if I know

when it was. Try to catch someone up in a lie." He scrolled through his contacts and hit a button. Ryan grinned as a voice came over his phone. "Trent, just the man I wanted to talk to. This is Detective Greer." He listened. "Yes, the one who brought in the recording device to see if you could find anything recorded over." His eyes widened. "Really? You did! Can you send it to me?" Ryan nodded. "That's good work. I also need you to see if you can find a time footprint on the computer. Yes. I need to know when…" He read the page of the manuscript from the recording before the argument. "No, I don't need a time, just a day. Thanks." He hung up the phone.

"That was a lab tech at the State Police Crime Lab. He uncovered what was recorded over and he is sure he can determine when this argument took place." Ryan finished off his ice cream in record time.

Shandra took his empty bowl and stood. "I'll clean up these dishes and then I'm going to bed."

"I'll be there after I get the recording from Trent. He said he'd email it to me."

She nodded and left him to his work. She'd had enough sleuthing today. While she was in the kitchen, Sheba woofed at the back door. Shandra let the animal in and headed to bed. Ryan had his attention on his laptop.

Shandra's soft footsteps barely registered as Ryan stared intently at the email from his buddy in Seattle about the Barsotti family. It appeared the new generation of Barsotti's had taken their predecessor's bootlegging and gambling to drug trafficking and human trafficking. From the way the current Vince Barsotti worked to keep his name and construction business legit, he wanted to keep all eyes off the activities he orchestrated at night.

But Ryan didn't understand how the elderly Mrs. Narvel could be a threat to Barsotti. The recording that had been erased talked about how Mr. Narvel had gone to a longtime friend, Mr. Barsotti, to be one of the backers of the ski resort. She talked as if it was all on the up and up. No mention of the family's ties to anything illegal. He had a feeling she didn't know the Barsotti legacy, but Holmes did. Ryan sent off an email to a PI he knew in Seattle, asking him to put out feelers if there had been any talk of someone trying to blackmail Mr. Barsotti. Then he sent off an email to Sheriff Oldham asking him to get a warrant for Mr. Jeffrey Holmes financial statements. If the writer was blackmailing someone, his financials would show large sums of income in the last few months.

He glanced at the clock on the wall. One a.m. He should get to bed. There were leads to follow in the morning and an interesting dinner to attend that night. A quick glance through his messages showed his mom had tried to contact him. He tapped that message.

"Ryan, we'd love to have you and Shandra join us for church and dinner tomorrow."

He shook his head. He wasn't bringing Shandra to a Sunday dinner at his parents. They'd be discussing wedding venues and the like. That would only scare Shandra off. She was getting closer to accepting he would stick with her no matter what, but she wasn't there yet, and he wasn't going to let his family do anything to undermine his progress.

Chapter Fourteen

Shandra woke Sunday morning feeling refreshed and almost normal. The antibiotics Dr. Porter prescribed were working. She made waffles and scrambled eggs for breakfast. Ryan wandered in, staring at his phone.

"What's wrong?" She placed a cup of steaming coffee on the counter at his usual spot.

"The tech says the argument was a week before the homicide. Why is there only a couple more recordings and only ten pages of manuscript after that?" He sat down and sipped his coffee.

She set his breakfast in front of him. "It is strange that there were only two sessions in a whole week." She sat down next to him. "We can ask Dr. Porter tonight when we have dinner. Maybe he knows why."

"That's a good plan. What did you want to do

today?" Ryan poured syrup on his waffles.

"You aren't working?"

"Since it's Sunday, everything I requested last night won't be available until tomorrow. I'm all yours. I'll question Dr. Porter and Mrs. Aducci tonight either before or after dinner." He chewed the waffle he'd put in his mouth.

"We could go for a horseback ride. We haven't done that since last fall." She'd been itching to get on her horse but with getting ready for the show and then the illness, she hadn't had the time or the energy to enjoy the sunshine and the spring flowers on the mountain.

"It's a date." Ryan put another forkful of waffle in his mouth.

Ryan had enjoyed the ride on the mountain with Shandra. It had given him a chance to relax and put all the things he knew in perspective. Right now, his mind was telling him that Dana Alvarez was the person who shoved Mrs. Narvel down the stairs. He just had to gather the evidence to prove it.

As he drove to Huckleberry, his mind wasn't all on business. Shandra sat beside him in his truck. When she'd walked out of her room, he'd just about picked her up and carried her back in. She was wearing the leggings that hugged her long athletic legs and a tunic that was flattering and sexy as hell. He'd told her once how good she looked in leggings and now she graced him with the view every time they had a date. Her tall black with teal embroidered cowboy boots with a three-inch heel gave the whole outfit and her a don't mess with me attitude. The same attitude that had caught his attention the day they'd met over a homicide.

He loved her cowboy boots, but had been informed he'd have to stuff his clothes in a dresser rather than her have to downsize or move her collection of boots. Seeing her in the pair tonight, he was willing to give up closet space.

"We're going to be early," Shandra said.

"I know. I'm hoping to talk with either Dr. Porter or Miranda's mom or both before dinner. I'd like to get the information before I enjoy myself."

She laughed. "Enjoy yourself? You're going to be asking questions and possibly even checking out the house. I know this is more than a casual dinner for you."

He rested a hand on her knee and gave it a squeeze. "You know me too well."

"I was hoping for a tour of the house. It is the most interesting house I've ever seen." She leaned against his shoulder. "Do you want me to do the nosing around while you talk?"

"You'd like that wouldn't you?" He kissed the top of her head. "No. You aren't getting out of my sight all night."

They arrived at the Narvel house forty-five minutes early. Shandra carried in the flowers and he carried the wine they'd picked up on the way through town.

Miranda answered the door. "Oh, you're early, but welcome. Come in." The tall woman always had a pleasant, welcoming appearance. Tonight was no exception. Although Ryan thought she actually had more of a glow.

Shandra hugged her friend. "Thank you for inviting us."

Dr. Porter appeared in the doorway to the parlor. "Welcome." He held out his hand to Ryan and smiled at Shandra as she released Miranda.

The two women entered the parlor, their heads together whispering.

"I have a feeling we'll have to entertain ourselves from the look of those two," Dr. Porter said, his eyes on Miranda.

Ryan knew the look in the man's eyes. He was in love. "If you don't mind, I have a couple more questions and some information for you."

Dr. Porter shifted all of his attention to Ryan. "Do you want to go someplace more private?"

"Not unless you have something to hide from Miranda." Ryan wondered how much about the murder the doctor had told his girlfriend. Especially, having a dinner party here less than a week after the incident.

"Here is fine." Dr. Porter led the way to a small bar that Ryan hadn't noticed in the room before.

"Was this here the other day?" he asked.

"Yes, and no." Dr. Porter handed him the tray with glasses and a bottle of wine and gave the bar a shove. It rolled into the wall, looking like the bottom of a beam in the wall.

"Was that part of the original house?" Ryan had an idea the oxygen canister might be hidden in a similar cubby hole.

"There is a similar pull out in all the rooms above this one in the same place." The doctor pulled the bar back out and placed the items Ryan had held back on top. "Wine or beer," he asked.

"Beer if you have it."

He plucked a bucket of ice with six beers sticking out of it from a shelf in the bar.

Ryan grabbed one.

"Would you ladies like a glass of wine?" Dr. Porter asked the still chatting women.

"Please," they said in unison.

Ryan studied the room, specifically, the beam that hid the bar. Two more floors, possibly three, where the canister could be hidden. If they found the canister, he had a feeling they'd get the killers fingerprints.

Dr. Porter led them out into the conservatory. Ryan noted he closed the doors, even though he said it didn't matter if Miranda heard what they were discussing.

"What did you want to ask?"

"Last week, did your aunt and the writer work every day?" Ryan sipped his beer and inhaled the humid earthy scent of the conservatory.

"Last week? No. I believe Mr. Holmes said something about needing to take care of business at home. He was gone from Monday until Friday or Saturday." Dr. Porter sipped his beer and studied Ryan. "Why? Did he kill my aunt?" Red started at the man's neck and slowly rose to his hairline. It had to suck for him in school. Every embarrassment, every angry thought, the whole world would know.

"I haven't ruled him out, but I was trying to figure out why there were only two recordings and manuscript entries last week. You just confirmed why. I'll have some answers tomorrow on whether or not the man was a factor in your aunt's death." Ryan wandered over and fingered the waxy leaf of a plant he'd never seen before.

"Have you come to any conclusions?" the doctor asked, following him deeper into the lush growth of tropical plants.

"Nothing concrete. I have my suspicions based on a recording Holmes made that was of an argument between your aunt and Dana Alvarez."

Dr. Porter faced him. "You think Dana did this?" He shook his head. "She's angry with the world and her father in particular, but I can't see her pushing Aunt Gladys down the stairs. She grew up in this house. My aunt thought of her as a niece." He took a sip of beer. "That was until she caught Dana stealing."

"In this argument, your aunt found Dana upstairs. She accused her of trying to steal more jewelry. Told her she wasn't welcome in this house any more. Dana came back with her mother lived here, and your aunt said her mother could be fired."

Dr. Porter sputtered. "I don't believe that. Aunt Gladys has had Mrs. Alvarez as her housekeeper ever since I was a child. I can't believe she would fire her because of Dana. It had to have been an idle threat to see if she could straighten Dana out."

Ryan had wondered how long the housekeeper

had worked here. This answered his questions.

The man was now paler than normal. Ryan didn't like how pale. Best to give him some good news. "We've determined that Miss Tapfer is a fake, and Mr. Holmes provided her with a false birth certificate. At this time, we're not sure if she was duped or was in on the scam."

"In my heart, I knew my aunt hadn't had a child. As much as she cherished family, she would have never given a child away."

"She did have a child as a teen. That was true."

"How? Who?" Dr. Porter dropped down on a padded bench between two small palm trees.

Ryan watched the man as he gave him the facts as they knew them. "I don't know who. She never gave a name. It appears to have been rape by a family member. She did go to a convent, where I believe her parents wanted her to give the child up for adoption. But the child died at two days old. All records were burned in a fire years ago, but we found a gravestone for May Alexandra Porter."

The doctor's head came up and he stared at Ryan. "May Alexandra? My father told me Aunt Gladys named me. Maynard Alexander. No wonder she was so willing to help me with everything and took me in summers. I was the child she lost." His eyes floated in unshed tears.

"Would you like me to send Miranda in here?" Ryan asked, easing toward the door.

The man nodded.

Ryan strode to the door and discovered Mr. and Mrs. Aducci had arrived. Shandra's gaze landed on him the minute he came through the door.

"Miranda, Alex would like to talk to you out in the conservatory."

Her eyes widened as she stood and hurried over to him.

In a low voice he said, "He had a shock with some information I told him. Let him tell you."

She nodded, then spun back to the room. "Momma, Poppa, I'll be few minutes." She disappeared into the conservatory.

Shandra didn't know what had happened, but if Ryan felt Dr. Porter needed Miranda then they were free to ask Mrs. Aducci questions.

Ryan crossed the room, shaking hands with both the Aduccis. "Nice to see you two out of the restaurant."

"It is good to have a night off now and then," Mr. Aducci said, raising his glass of wine and sitting back down on the couch next to his wife.

"Mr. and Mrs. Aducci were just telling us about their recent trip to Seattle. Their son, Tony, lives there with his wife and two children." Shandra said, bringing up the town were Mr. Barsotti lived. She wasn't sure how Ryan planned to get to that.

"From the smiles on your faces the trip was good," Ryan said.

"It was! We played with the grandchildren and saw our son's restaurant." Mrs. Aducci beamed with happiness.

Mr. Aducci didn't seem as pleased. "It is a rip-off!"

"What do you mean?" Shandra asked.

"They charge twice what our most expensive meal is and put two little things on the plate. He is no longer a chef, he is a con artist."

Shandra giggled. "That is what the people of Seattle like."

"That is what is wrong with that city. Too much corruption. Why he chooses to live and raise his family where there is so much dishonesty, I do not know." Mr. Aducci frowned and swallowed the rest of his wine.

Shandra rose, walked to the bar, and picked up the wine bottle. She refilled Mr. Aducci's glass. "This is a beautiful house," she said to bring the conversation away from the older man's rant. "Have you been in it before?" she asked Mrs. Aducci.

"Yes, when we first moved here, Mr. Narvel and Gladys kept us here until we found the right place for our restaurant and to live." She dabbed a handkerchief at her eyes. "I was sad to hear of her passing when we returned." She lowered her voice. "And that we were invited to dinner here so soon after her passing."

"Miranda and Dr. Porter have become good friends," Shandra said, wondering if the couple had any clue what was about to happen.

"This is news to us!" Mr. Aducci said.

"I had noticed the doctor coming to eat at the restaurant more since before Christmas." Mrs. Aducci smiled. "I think he and my Miranda are a lovely couple."

Mr. Aducci humphed.

Shandra had never seen the normally cordial

man so out of sorts.

"You said you stayed with the Narvels when you first planned a business here. How did you know them?" Ryan asked.

It was about time he jumped into the conversation. Shandra smiled at Ryan.

"I knew Gladys Porter in Portland. Her family were high society. They had parties and hosted charity balls. My mother helped in the kitchen during these things." Mrs. Aducci smiled. "Miss Gladys always had a smile and a laugh for anyone. She didn't have the airs her parents and brother had."

"What happened when she married Mr. Narvel?" Ryan asked.

"Oh, he moved Gladys to Seattle. They lived there five or six years then moved here." She shook her head. "Even though Gladys didn't have airs, I couldn't believe when I'd heard she'd moved to such a small place. She liked to throw parties and socialize."

"I wondered about that too," Shandra said. "Did Mr. Narvel have the idea of a ski resort before he headed here?"

"I don't know. I'd lost touch with her until she called and said they were building the ski resort and the town could use a good Italian restaurant. She said her husband would finance our start. We were struggling with all the restaurants in Portland and decided to give it a try. We have been here forty-four years and have nothing to complain about. Our children were raised here, and we've had a good life."

"Did Mr. Narvel finance many of the businesses that first went in?" Ryan asked.

"Yes. Our restaurant, two others, Maxine's only it was a different owner. The grocery store and one of the quick marts. And he built the lodge and ski run. He was most generous." Mrs. Aducci nodded her head.

Mr. Aducci shook his head.

"Why are you shaking your head, Mr. Aducci?" Shandra asked.

"My wife thinks Mr. Narvel was generous. She did not make the payments to him. Yes, he loaned us money to start up, and didn't ask us to start paying back until we were making a profit. But he asked us to use his bank for all deposits and bill paying." Mr. Aducci shook his finger. "It was not armored trucks who brought his money in and out. They were brown vans with men in regular clothes carrying guns in holsters under their jackets."

Shandra understood what the man was saying. Huckleberry was sustained in the early days by mob money. She glanced over at Ryan and saw the same thoughts going through his head.

"When was the local bank bought out by the corporate one that is here now?" Ryan asked.

"Ten-twelve years ago. Whenever the last payments were made on the businesses." Mr. Aducci sipped his wine. "That was the best thing that could have happened to the Huckleberry businesses."

Dr. Porter and Miranda returned from the

conservatory. They were holding hands. Miranda smiled but it wasn't the same glow she'd displayed earlier. Dr. Porter's eyes were sunken and his pale complexion looked more sallow than white. What had he and Ryan talked about? Was he the killer, and he wanted to tell Miranda before anyone else did? Shandra's heart ached for her friend and raced with anxiety at the thought of Dr. Porter being a murderer. Was that what her dream had meant?

"Mr. and Mrs. Aducci, welcome to my aunt- I mean my home. I'm glad you could join us." Dr. Porter led Miranda over to sit next to her mother and he moved to the bar, refilling the wine glasses and handing Ryan another beer.

Mrs. Alvarez appeared in the door of the parlor. "Dinner is served."

"Thank you, Mrs. Alvarez." Dr. Porter returned to Miranda's side, offering her his arm. She slid her hand over his arm and they led the rest of them into the dining room.

Shandra could see Miranda hosting parties and business dinners here. She bumped into Ryan, holding him in the hall while the others were seated. "What happened with Dr. Porter? Did he confess?"

"No. I told him about his aunt and the cousin who died. He seemed devastated at the news. I'll tell you more later." He escorted her into the room and deposited her in the seat next to Miranda at one end of the table. Dr. Porter sat at the opposite end, the Aducci's were on Miranda's right and Shandra and Ryan were on her left.

"Help yourselves. Mrs. Alvarez is a very good

cook," Dr. Porter said, himself sitting in his chair, staring at Miranda.

When everyone had food on their plates, Miranda cleared her throat. "Momma, Poppa, Alex and I asked you here tonight to tell you we have been dating and…" Her hopeful tone faltered.

"I had planned to ask your permission to marry your daughter. But history I learned tonight makes me think we should slow down and rethink marriage." Dr. Porter raised his glass to Miranda. "Your daughter is beautiful inside and out. I love her, but I don't want to burden her with my family legacy."

Mrs. Aducci had been smiling until he mentioned the family legacy. "What legacy?"

"Alex is afraid he won't be able to find a cure for the disease the male heirs in his family carry. He doesn't want to leave me a widow." She grasped Shandra's hand. "He's pigheaded. I told him I would rather spend the next twelve years with him and know we had lived happy than have him kick me to the side now and he finds a cure after I've settled for someone else."

"She has a point," Shandra said, squeezing her friend's hand.

"I agree. You can't live your life dreading what may or may not happen," Mrs. Aducci said.

Dr. Porter waved at the men on either side of him. "What do you think? Better to let Miranda move on in case I don't find the cure or marry and wonder how she'll survive, possibly with children who may carry the same gene?"

Ryan glanced at Shandra and said. "I'd think whatever days you have with someone you love is better than being alone." His right hand settled on her leg.

Shandra smiled and glanced at Mr. Aducci.

"You're a doctor. You fix people." Mr. Aducci stared at his daughter. "My Miranda has a big heart, she fixes people too. Her kindness is a gift. If you have benefited from her love and wish to throw it away, you are not the smart man I thought you were." He lifted his glass of wine. "A toast to Dr. Porter and my daughter, Miranda. May you live long, love often, and give us many more grandchildren!"

Shandra laughed, and raised her glass. Everyone shouted "Hear! Hear!"

Dr. Porter slowly raised his glass, his eyes on Miranda. "I guess this is one time I need to listen and not accept what my mind is telling me."

Miranda sprang out of her chair, knocking it over and ran to Dr. Porter. "Does this mean the engagement will happen?"

He slid out of his chair and down on one knee. Dr. Porter grasped her hand and pulled a ring out of a jacket pocket. "Miranda Arnella Aducci, will you marry me?"

"Yes!" She pulled him to his feet, and they kissed before he even put the ring on her finger.

Shandra glanced at Ryan. He was watching her. They shared a brief moment of sizing up the others reaction to the event before Miranda's parents jumped up and hugged the engaged couple. Shandra found the moment touching and was glad she was a part of it, but she hoped when Ryan asked her, it was just the two of them. Not a big display for family or friends.

After dinner, Shandra asked the question she'd been wanting to ask since the drive over. "I love this house. Is there a chance I can get a tour?"

Dr. Porter smiled. "I love this house, too. Coming here as a child, I thought my aunt lived in a castle. Mr. and Mrs. Aducci, would you like a tour?"

"No, we need to get home. Tomorrow is the day we drive to Coeur d'Alene for supplies." Mr. Aducci shook hands with the men and kissed Shandra and his daughter on the cheek. Mrs. Aducci hugged everyone and they walked out the front door.

"You've seen the dining room and parlor. Shandra follow me. I'll show you the conservatory and library before we go to the second floor."

She fell in beside Dr. Porter as he told her about each room and the bit of history he knew about them. She marveled at the craftsmanship and décor.

"My aunt did all the decorating herself. It was her hobby."

They climbed the stairs. Shandra shivered as they moved higher up. At the top, a chill rippled through her. This is where Mrs. Narvel knew she would die. Shandra moved closer to Ryan. He put an arm around her as if he understood her need for comfort.

"This was my aunt's room," Dr. Porter said, opening the door at the top and to the left of the stairs.

The room looked like a photo from a 1940's movie.

"This is like stepping back in time," Shandra stepped into the room and immediately felt welcome.

"When Miranda and I marry, this will be our room. I'm going to have the small bedroom at the top of the stairs made into a master bathroom." Dr. Porter reached out for Miranda's hand.

She smiled and moved closer. "I love the room just the way it is."

He shook his head. "You can redecorate. I don't want it to remind me of Aunt Gladys."

"I understand." She kissed his cheek and they moved out of the room.

"That's where Jeffrey was staying until I kicked him out this morning. I think he took all of his belongings." Dr. Porter opened the door. The room had yet to be cleaned. The bed was unmade, and he'd left the room trashed.

"My goodness! I don't think he was happy you kicked him out." Miranda walked around the room, picking things up.

"Do you know where he went?" Ryan asked.

"I have the address downstairs. He wanted mail forwarded." Dr. Porter walked over to a beam that resembled the one by the bar in the parlor.

"This is the other cubby hole you were asking about," he said to Ryan.

The man tugged on the beam and a drawer four feet high and as wide as the beam rolled out. Shandra looked down into the drawer. Extra linens were stored in it.

"That is fantastic! Did your aunt have that made?" she asked.

"No. They discovered it after they moved in. She thought they were wonderful conversation pieces." Dr. Porter stopped Miranda from tidying up the room. "Mrs. Alvarez will see to this room tomorrow. With only me living here now she has lots of free time on her hands."

He walked through a door next to the closet, and they were in another bedroom. "This is where I slept in the summers until I was thirteen. Then I started sleeping on the third floor, which is where I stay now."

They had a quick look at the quaint but updated bathroom before they went up another flight of stairs.

"That is the bath at the end of the hall. He opened a door to the right of the stairs. "This is where I sleep."

He'd led them into a dark masculine room. Heavy furniture and everything neat and tidy. She hoped Miranda could loosen the man up. Even Ryan left shoes here or a tie there which made the room feel lived in and shared.

"And this—"

Ryan stopped him with a hand on his arm. "Is there a hiding compartment in this room as well?" He nodded toward the beam like the one on the last two stories.

"Yes. But I can tell you, all you'll find in there are items from my youth I decided to keep." Dr. Porter walked across the room and gave the beam a tug.

Curious to see what a man like Dr. Porter would keep from his childhood, Shandra gasped at the shiny stainless steel canister in the drawer.

Chapter Fifteen

Ryan put a hand on Dr. Porter's arm when he started to reach in and grab the oxygen canister. "Don't touch that." He didn't want to believe the doctor had killed his aunt, but finding what Ryan considered key evidence in the murder in the doctor's room was damaging.

"Miranda, take Alex down to the parlor. Shandra, go to the basement kitchen and ask Mrs. Alvarez for a garbage sack, please."

Both women did as they were told.

"I didn't put that there. I open that drawer maybe once a year," Dr. Porter said as Miranda led him out of the room.

Ryan pulled out his phone and dialed Sheriff's dispatch.

"Weippe County Sheriff's Department," said Charles Wyland.

"Charles, this is Ryan. I've discovered the missing oxygen tank. I believe the fingerprints will tell us the suspect in Mrs. Narvel's death. I need a deputy to come to the Narvel house, pick it up, and take it to the state lab."

"I believe Speaks is in your area. I'll radio and let him know."

"Thank you." Ryan disconnected and decided to make an informal investigation of the doctor's room.

~*~

Shandra found the stairs to the basement and hurried down, bursting through the door and into the light of the kitchen. Mrs. Alvarez and the young woman she'd spotted watching the day of the murder, jumped up from where they sat at a table.

"I'm sorry, I didn't mean to scare you. I need a garbage bag." She walked into the room and held her hand out to the young woman. "Shandra Higheagle, I don't think we've met."

"Dana." The woman didn't shake hands.

"What do you need a garbage bag for?" Mrs. Alvarez asked, pulling one out of a cupboard.

"It's for Detective Greer. I don't know why he wants it." She grabbed the bag and headed to the stairs, but not before seeing a look between the two.

She huffed up the first flight, the second flight, and stopped in the doorway of the doctor's bedroom. It was empty. She walked over to the drawer. The canister was still in the drawer.

"Ryan?" she called.

He stepped into the room. "I was next door in

what appears to be Dr. Porter's office. All his research papers are neatly bound and stacked. Nothing out of the ordinary in there." He had on plastic gloves.

"Where did you get those?" She pointed to his hands.

"Knowing we were coming here and you would be curious, I put a pair in my pocket just in case we ran into this." He picked up the canister. "Open the bag."

She held the bag open and he placed the canister inside. "Do you think Dr. Porter killed his aunt?"

"I don't know. But from marks on the victim, I believe whoever did, pulled this from the woman before she fell down the stairs. Which would mean their fingerprints could be on it. And whoever it was had to know about the hiding places in this beam."

"People who live in this house." Shandra thought of the two women in the kitchen. "Dana and her mother were in the kitchen just now. Mrs. Alvarez asked why I needed a bag. I told her you wanted it."

"And what did she say to that?" He took the bag from her.

"Nothing. But they shared a conspiratorial look."

He grinned. "It could be because one or both of them put the canister in the drawer. Come on. I need to question Dr. Porter."

Shandra followed him down the two sets of stairs to the parlor.

Dr. Porter and Miranda sat on the couch. His arm around her waist, her arm around his shoulders. Shandra hoped for her friend's sake, the doctor's prints weren't on the canister.

Ryan placed the bagged canister inside the parlor door. "Dr. Porter, when was the last time you touched this canister?"

The pale man looked up. His brow furrowed as he thought.

Miranda rubbed his back with her hand.

"I took it from my aunt the night before her death, when she came down to dinner. We were standing at the hall closet where her first floor concentrator is installed. She took off the canister, and I hung it from the hook in the closet while she attached the nasal cannula from the concentrator."

"Did you help her with her canister when she retired for the night?" Ryan asked.

Dr. Porter shook his head. "I went out." He glanced at Miranda. "I don't know if anyone helped her. She pretty much did everything unless I was here. She didn't trust the others to know how to help. Aunt Gladys called it her medical miracle that kept her alive and I was the only one who knew how to operate it properly." He shook his head. "Even though most of the time all I ever did was hang up or hand her the canister. Anyone could do that."

A knock at the front door had everyone looking toward the hall.

"That should be Deputy Speaks. I'm having him take the canister to the lab to be checked for fingerprints." Ryan picked up the bag with the canister and answered the door.

"You wanted me to pick up something," Gerald Speaks asked.

"Yes. Take this to the state lab. If they can accelerate the results, I'd be grateful. Two of my suspects could be headed out of town soon." Ryan handed over the bag.

"Will do. Anything else?"

"If Sheriff Oldham comes through with a warrant tomorrow, the sooner it gets here the better."

Speaks grinned. "Not a problem."

Ryan bid the deputy good night and returned to the parlor.

Shandra sat in a chair watching the two on the couch. She glanced up as he walked into the room.

"Sorry to end such a nice evening on a sour note." Ryan held out his hand to Shandra. She grasped his fingers and he helped her to her feet.

"Yes, I'm sorry, too. Once Ryan gets the fingerprints off the canister, he'll know who to go after." Shandra said, walking over to the couch and leaning to hug Miranda. "Congratulations."

Miranda gave her a half smile. "Thanks."

Dr. Porter stood. "I'll take you home," he said to Miranda.

"We can drop her," Shandra offered.

Ryan could tell the doctor wanted time alone with the woman. "Shandra, let the man take his fiancée home." He reclaimed Shandra's hand, leading her to the door.

She paused as he opened the door. "I guess they want to be alone, don't they?"

"Wouldn't you if I'd just proposed to you?" He held the door and she walked out.

"I think it's more because of us finding that canister in his room. He was really quiet and withdrawn since finding it."

He noticed how she'd skipped right over his comment about proposing to her. One of these days, he hoped she would allow herself to dig into the conversation. "Quiet, how? Like 'shit I've been caught' or 'There's only one person who could have done this'?"

"The later. Like he was piecing things together in his mind." She climbed in the driver's side when he opened the door.

His heart picked up pace as he slid in and she remained close. He started the vehicle and headed down the driveway.

"Do you honestly think he killed an aunt you can tell he loved very much?"

"I've seen mothers kill their children and children kill their mothers. I've seen the sweetest of old ladies off her husband of sixty years. Sometimes there is a trigger in people that snaps and they kill someone they love for the dumbest of reasons." He shook his head. "I've never been able to figure it out."

She slipped her arms around his arm and snuggled against him. "Let's think of something pleasant. The dinner was nice. Mrs. Alvarez is a good cook. I can't believe Mrs. Narvel would have fired her."

"Dr. Porter thinks it was just a ploy by his aunt to try and straighten Dana out. He said the girl has lived at the house her whole life and his aunt considered her a niece."

"So, she was doing tough love with her."

"That's what Dr. Porter thought." Ryan put his hand on her leg. "We're still talking about the case."

"Sorry. I enjoyed our horseback ride today."

He smiled. "Me too. There's nothing like a ride in the woods to get things put into perspective. It was relaxing." And he'd figured out where he would propose to Shandra when the time was right.

~*~

Shandra walked along the edge of a cliff. Fear speared her chest. Miranda stood on the opposite side, her body leaning over the open chasm. Dr. Porter was hanging from a root on the side of the cliff. Miranda couldn't reach him, she was too far away to help, and Ryan stood at the bottom, hollering for the man to jump. Shandra called up to Ella, "Help him!" She shook her head and pointed behind Miranda. A shadowy figure stood back watching all that was unfolding. She tried to focus on the figure but fog rolled in, hiding the person.

She sat up in bed. The dream had felt real. Why had Ryan called to Dr. Porter to jump when it had been a hundred feet or better? And what of the shadowy person? Was there someone from Dr. Porter's life who wished him dead as well as his aunt?

Chapter Sixteen

Shandra sat at the counter making a list of things she needed to get done this week for the event she was attending in one week. She hoped Mrs. Narvel's death was solved by then. She didn't like the idea of leaving here without knowing what had happened.

Ryan had left early, wanting to be close to the people he wanted to question when he had all the information he'd asked for over the weekend.

Shandra was positive Dr. Porter had nothing to do with his aunt's death. The shadowy person in her dream was the killer. The person had stood back, watching Dr. Porter hanging on for his life from the cliff. As if they'd taken out Mrs. Narvel and wanted to take out the doctor as well.

That meant there had to be someone else in line for the inheritance. She knew Mrs. Narvel's baby had died. As well as her brother who was the doctor's father. What about cousins? Was there a relative out there somewhere that no one knew about?

She shoved her list away from her. There was one person in Huckleberry who knew Mrs. Narvel's life. But she and her husband were headed to Coeur d'Alene. She picked up her phone to see if there was a way to meet with Mrs. Aducci today.

"Hello?" Miranda answered, not sounding a bit like her cheery self.

"Hi. I hate to bother you this morning, but I was wondering if there would be a chance to see your mom today." She had a notion the newly engaged couple had a long night of worrying.

"She and Pop usually have breakfast at Ruthies before they head out." Her voice faded and returned. "They'll be getting there in the next thirty minutes."

"Good. Can you call and ask them to wait for me to get there? I have a couple of questions for your mom."

"My mom? What about?" Miranda's tone held suspicion.

"Nothing about you or Alex. I want to know more about Mrs. Narvel. I think someone, possibly family, is trying to frame Alex."

"He doesn't have any other family." Miranda insisted.

"That he knows of. There could be some distant relative that decided it was time to cash in on the family money." Shandra hurried to the bedroom and shoved her feet into her every day boots. "Call her. I'm on my way."

She dropped her phone into her purse, grabbed a light jacket, and whistled for Sheba as she walked to the barn to pull out her Jeep.

"Where are you going? You got vases to crate." Lil said, walking in from the corrals at the back of the barn.

"I know. I have some questions for Mrs. Aducci. I'll grab breakfast while I'm talking with her and be back by eleven at the latest. We'll crate the vases then and pack the other items I'll need."

Lil huffed. "This is the first time you've put off getting ready for a show. I told you havin' that policeman livin' here is bad for your business."

Shandra shook her head. "He's good for my creativity. I'll be back before noon, I promise."

Sheba jumped in the back seat before the door was all the way open. Shandra laughed and said, "I guess you wanted to ride along pretty bad."

She started the vehicle and headed down her driveway faster than was prudent given the potholes and rocks she didn't bother smoothing out. Out on the county road she drove ten miles an hour over her usual pace fearing if the Aducci's had to wait too long for her they would leave.

~*~

Ryan held the warrant in his hand as he spoke on the phone with the bank where Jeffrey Holmes banked. "I need to get the past twelve months of Jeffrey Holmes bank statements." He rattled off the warrant number, the judge, county, and description of what the warrant asked of the bank.

"We'll email you the statement," said the bank representative.

Ryan ended that call and his phone buzzed. The officer he'd asked to look into Barsotti was calling. He opened the connection and wandered into one of the questioning rooms. He didn't want to upset anyone with the questions he wanted answered.

"Darrel, what did you come up with?" Ryan asked.

"I couldn't find anyone who would say if Barsotti was hit with any blackmail. All of his legit and illegal operations seem to be running fine. No large withdrawals that aren't pulled every month for business. I don't think anyone was blackmailing him. I couldn't find anywhere that your suspect came to Seattle in the time period you mentioned."

Damn! He was sure Holmes could be held for more than counterfeiting the birth certificate. "Thanks. I owe you a few drinks the next time I see you."

"Count on it."

The line went silent.

His gut had told him Holmes was up to more than getting his girlfriend into the family money. Even though Darrel said there wasn't any noticeable changes in Barsotti's bank statement, Ryan opened his computer and email. There was the information from the bank. He pulled up the file and started skimming the pages.

He stopped at December of last year. Twenty thousand had been deposited in Holmes' account.

He wrote down the numbers and called the bank. After being shuffled from one representative to the next and finally getting a manager, he knew the money had been transferred from an account in Nevada. He set about contacting that bank and discovering who had sent Holmes the large sum.

~*~

Shandra parked in front of Ruthie's and hurried in, pleased to see Mrs. Aducci sitting in a booth. As she walked up she noted the woman appeared to be alone, there wasn't a second cup of coffee or plate at the table.

"Mrs. Aducci, are you alone?" Shandra slid into the booth across from the woman.

"Yes. Miranda said you needed to talk to me to help her Alex, so she went shopping with her father today." The older woman picked up a piece of toast and bit into it.

A teenaged waitress arrived. "Can I get you something."

"I'll have hot chocolate and biscuits and gravy please." She waited for the girl to leave before leaning forward. With her voice low, to keep others from hearing, she asked, "Did Mrs. Narvel have any distant relatives who might receive the inheritance if something happens to Dr. Porter?"

Mrs. Aducci sucked coffee in and started coughing.

Shandra sprang out of her side and patted the woman on the back. "I guess I should have eased into that question." When the woman had caught her breath, Shandra sat back down.

"She did have a cousin on her mother's side. I believe she was ten or fifteen years younger than Gladys." Mrs. Aducci stared over her shoulder. "They didn't visit very much. The sisters, Gladys' mother and her sister, didn't get along. Mrs. Porter married well and her sister didn't. I believe the sister's husband either ended up dead from a fight or in prison. I can't remember which."

"Where did they live? Do you remember their names?" Shandra had her phone out with her note taking app open.

Mrs. Aducci tapped a finger against her lips. "I believe the sister's name was Mabel, the daughter, Gladys' cousin, Jennifer or Judith, I can't remember."

"What about a last name, the sister's married name?" Shandra wasn't hopeful that they had much to go on.

"I don't remember the last name. I only knew the little bits Momma would tell us after she'd helped with a party. When I helped with parties, I think the sisters had been estranged for several years. I never heard anyone mention them." Mrs. Aducci studied her. "Does any of this help?"

"It gives me a starting point. Do you remember where they lived?"

"Portland."

"That should help some. Thank you for meeting with me."

The waitress arrived with her hot chocolate and her biscuits and gravy.

Ruthie walked out of the kitchen a few minutes

later with a cup of coffee in her hands. She slid into the booth alongside of Shandra. "Mrs. Aducci, I can't believe you ditched your loving man for Shandra."

The older woman laughed. "He needed a day with his daughter." She winked at Shandra. "There are going to be some changes in our family soon, and he needs to realize it."

Ruthie set her coffee down and glanced between Shandra and Mrs. Aducci. "What are you talking about?"

A big smile lit up the older woman's face. "Our Miranda is engaged!"

"Congratulations! Who is the lucky man?" Ruthie asked.

"Dr. Porter. He will be good for her." Mrs. Aducci nodded.

Ruthie faced Shandra. "Dr. Porter? But he just lost his aunt and…" She didn't finish.

Shandra knew what she was thinking, given their conversation last week. "They are very happy. It is helping him ease his grief over his aunt." She was itching to get to a computer and start searching for Mrs. Narvel's cousin.

Ryan had the name of the person who sent the money to Holmes. Genevieve Shaw. He opened up the public database and typed in the first name.

His phone buzzed.

The lab.

"Greer."

"We found fingerprints on the canister, three

sets, but none of them are in any of our systems. I sent them off to AFIS. I can tell you the set that is the most obscured came from a larger hand than the other two. That's about it. Sorry I couldn't give you better news."

"Thanks. If one of them is in AFIS, we'll know in a couple of days." He ended the conversation. Because none of the fingerprints were picked up in the local database, Dana Alvarez was no longer a suspect. He could see her lashing out without thinking which would mean she wouldn't have had gloves on to keep her fingerprints from getting on the canister. But three sets. He figured the larger more obscured prints were Dr. Porter's. Two other people had handled the canister besides him. One of the sets should match the victim. He picked up the phone and called the coroner.

"Sheila, did you take prints on Mrs. Narvel, my murder victim from Huckleberry?" he asked as soon as the coroner answered her phone.

"I did."

"Could you send them to the print lab and have them see if they match a set on an oxygen canister I sent over Saturday night."

"Will do."

He disconnected that call and dialed the sheriff's dispatch.

"Weippe County—"

"I know Cathleen. I called you." Ryan said just to fluster his older sister. "I need you to get on the Public Database and search for a Genevieve Shaw in Nevada. I need to know if she has a connection with Mrs. Narvel the murder victim, or Jeffrey Holmes of Sunset, California.”

"That could take a while with so little information." She sounded skeptical.

"You can find her. And when you do send me the information, I'm going to pick up someone for forgery." He disconnected the call. He'd rather be rousting Holmes than staring at a computer screen for hours.

He walked out of the room and straight to Blane. The young officer needed to learn proper etiquette on bringing in someone to question.

"Blane, you're coming with me." Ryan kept on walking as the officer jumped to his feet and tapped out a hurried cadence behind him.

Chapter Seventeen

Shandra was home by eleven. She parked in front of the house and hurried in to get on her computer. She pulled up newspapers from Portland, Oregon in the 1960's and started searching wedding announcements for women named Mabel and any reference to the Porters of high society.

She'd been at the search an hour when Lil stomped in the back door and down the hall to the main room. "I thought you said we'd crate up those vases when you came back?"

Shandra sighed and closed the lid on her laptop. "You aren't going to leave me alone until I do."

"You're darn right. Someone has to keep a level head around here when you're walking around with yours in the clouds." Lil pivoted and stomped back outside.

Laughing, Shandra followed the venting

woman and entered the studio. Three crates sat on the floor, a large bag of shredded wood shavings sat beside them. Lil had everything set up to get the vases ready for transport.

"When we get these done, I'll take the crates down to the freight office and send them to the convention center." Lil bent to put shavings in the bottom of the smallest wood crate. The woman had helped her enough times that she could do the packing herself, but she wanted Shandra to be able to say without a doubt that her vases were in one piece when they were shipped. She'd had one vase arrive at a show in a dozen pieces.

She began the task of wrapping the smallest vase in bubble wrap while Lil made a shaving nest in the crate.

~*~

Ryan pulled up to the Chalet Lodge Motel with Blane. He scanned the parking lot for Holmes' car. "Do you have the plate number of Jeffrey Holmes' vehicle?" he asked Blane.

The officer spouted the number without checking a log book.

"I don't see it. Do you have a make and license for Miss Tapfer's car?" he asked, scanning the parking lot, assessing the cars.

Again, the young officer gave the information out of his head and not off a notepad. Perhaps this intelligence was why Chief Sandberg kept the over-zealous officer around.

Ryan glanced over the cars. "Her car isn't here either. I told them both not to leave town." He parked his vehicle and entered the motel office. He'd interrogated the owner before.

"I don't want no trouble," the man said, his jowly face taking on a red hue.

"There won't be any trouble. Can you tell me what happened to Mr. Jeffrey Holmes and Miss Tapfer?" Ryan leaned on the counter as Blane stood by the door, acting like he'd keep anyone from bolting out.

"Never had no one by the name of Holmes here lately. The Tapfer woman checked out this morning." The manager said, eyeing Ryan and then Blane.

"Did the woman say if she was going home?"

"No, she said she was staying in the area. Just getting better accommodations. Can you believe that? Told me straight to my face she was going to stay in a nicer place." He held up his hands and looked around. "What's wrong with this motel? Clean beds, away from the noisy street."

Ryan shook his head. It was also the place the police were called the most for drunken parties and domestic assaults.

"Come on," he said to Blane, moving the younger man out of the way so he could leave the office. Once they were both in the SUV he said, "We'll cruise around. Keep an eye out for either of the cars."

Blane nodded and Ryan headed the vehicle back to the main road and out toward the ski lodge. There were half a dozen better class of motels along the road and there was also the lodge. Though he wondered at either Holmes or the woman having the money to stay for very long at the lodge.

That was where they found both cars. Parked side by side in the Huckleberry Lodge parking lot. Where would either of them have found the means to stay here? Ryan parked his SUV.

"Stay here and watch their cars. If you see either of them, call me and apprehend. I want a word with both of them."

"Yes, sir." Blane needed little incentive when it came to apprehending a suspect.

Ryan exited the vehicle and walked up the steps and into the lodge. It was as opulent as his first visit here two years before when Shandra was on his suspect list. He went straight to the check-in desk.

He pulled out his badge and made his introduction to the middle-aged woman behind the counter. "I need to know if you have either a Jeffrey Holmes or a Genie Tapfer staying here."

The woman eyed him skeptically. "We don't give out the names or rooms of the people staying with us."

"Call Doring or Ms. Gamble, please." He stood at the counter, waiting for the woman to pick up the phone. He'd had run-ins with the owner Sidney Doring several times, but he liked Meredith Gamble, Shandra's friend who ran the lodge.

The woman paused a moment before picking up the phone and poking three numbers. He bet she'd picked the manager over the owner.

"Ms. Gamble, there is a detective here to speak

with you." She listened then nodded. "Yes. I will." She placed the receiver back on the phone and pointed down the hall. "She said you can catch her as she comes out of the kitchen."

Ryan strode in the direction of the lodge kitchen. He knew the location of the 'employee only' door from using it at one time while keeping three steps ahead of state police officers trying to tag Shandra with the murder of her ex-lover.

He reached the door at the same time Ms. Gamble stepped out. She pushed her horn-rimmed glasses tighter on her round face and smiled. "Detective, how is Shandra? I haven't seen her since the show last summer."

Ryan enjoyed seeing how the people of Huckleberry cared for Shandra. She may not have grown up here, but they had taken her in as if she had. "She's fine. Getting over the cold that has been going around."

She started walking, and he fell into step beside her. "What is it you need from me?"

"Your help. I asked if you had a couple of people staying here who are part of an investigation, but the woman at the desk wouldn't tell me." He tried to look apologetic for the woman's employee having dragged Ms. Gamble into the conversation.

"It is against policy to give out our customers' names but not when it's law enforcement." She walked into her office and Ryan followed. "What are their names?" She poised her hand over a keyboard.

"Holmes and Tapfer."

She held her hands in place. "The nice couple who registered this morning?" Her face froze in horror. "You want them for something illegal?"

"I want them for questioning."

"Did they do something bad?" she asked, this time typing the names to find the room.

"I don't know at this point." He didn't want to tell the woman more than necessary. She didn't appear to be a gossip but in this community word spread faster than fire fueled by fifty-mile-an-hour winds.

"They are in room two-forty-three."

"They?"

"Yes. I said couple." She peered at him through her thick lenses, her eyes not blinking.

"Thank you." He stood and headed to the door.

"Are they a danger to our other clientele?"

"No."

She nodded and he headed to the elevators. Hopefully the two were in their room. This confirmed his information that the two had known one another before they cooked up the story of Miss Tapfer being Mrs. Narvel's granddaughter. But had they resorted to murder to get the money?

~*~

Shandra was back at the computer as soon as Lil disappeared down the driveway with the crates. She sipped her tea and read the social pages of the newspapers as well as the crime column.

Her heart started racing when she ran across a wedding announcement that had a Mrs. Edward Narvel formerly, Miss Gladys Porter, standing up for Miss Mabel Shaw as she married Dwight Grun. Mrs. Narvel had been at her cousin's wedding. This made Shandra wonder if the two had corresponded through the years. Their mothers were the ones who had the falling out.

She had names. She wrote down Mabel Shaw Grun and Dwight Grun. She continued to scan the births and crime columns. She wanted to know if there were any children and when Dwight ended up in jail.

Her eyes were going cross-eyed when she noted the time. Ryan would be home for dinner soon. She had names to give him. He could put them in his database and probably pop the rest of the information out quicker than her scanning the old newspapers.

Dream a Little Dream chimed from her phone. She picked it up and smiled. Ryan.

"Hello. I was just getting ready to make dinner."

"I won't be there until late. I'm questioning suspects." He sounded as tired as she felt.

"Are you getting sick?" she asked, worrying she'd shared her strep throat.

"No, exasperated. I know Holmes and Tapfer are lying but I can't catch them up in it." He sighed heavily. "Don't wait up for me."

Chapter Eighteen

Ryan closed his connection to Shandra and sat at Blane's desk, rereading the information he had on Holmes and Tapfer. They hadn't been happy to find him outside their room at the lodge and even less happy to be escorted to the Huckleberry P.D. Right now, they were stone-walling him.

He had to find something that would get them talking. He'd start with the forged birth certificate and Miss Tapfer. He picked up the file with the certificate and the report of it being illegitimate and headed to question the woman, again.

Miss Tapfer looked up from picking at her nails. Her face was blank, unlike the anger that had crossed it when Holmes had opened the door at the lodge.

"I don't understand why you have dragged us back in here," she said, returning her gaze to her hands folded on the table.

"I'm still looking for who murdered Mrs. Narvel and I have questions about this." He pulled the birth certificate out of the folder and slid it across the table.

"My mother's birth certificate. Why?" She was either a very good liar or Holmes hadn't told her it was a forgery.

"This is a forgery. I don't believe your mother was Mrs. Narvel's daughter."

She didn't answer.

"I'll know soon enough. We're searching the records on you. Would you care to tell me how you allowed Mr. Holmes to pull you into this?"

She slowly raised her head and stared into his eyes. "I tried to tell him it wouldn't work. But he said the woman, Mrs. Narvel, was so family crazy she wouldn't dig into whether or not it was true once she saw the certificate. I swear, all I wanted was to make Jeffrey happy and live in comfort the rest of my life." A tear glistened in one eye. "I would have made her happy. I never knew my grandmother, but I'd always wanted one."

He slipped the paper back in the file and stood. "I'll be back." He didn't for one minute believe her tears. Someone paid Mr. Holmes either for blackmail or for pushing this woman off as the victim's granddaughter.

Blane stood outside the questioning room where Holmes was waiting.

"Watch this room. I don't want her fleeing." Ryan nodded to the room he'd left.

The officer nodded.

Ryan entered the smaller room and found Jeffrey Holmes' knee bouncing and his eyes wide and wild.

"Why did you haul us in here like criminals?" he asked, immediately taking a belligerent stand.

"Because you are." He slid the forged birth certificate across the table. "This is fake."

"You told me that last time. If you're going to press charges, do it." Even as he challenged, his eyes didn't hold the same bravado. He appeared scared.

"I want to know who paid you the twenty thousand that showed up in your back account."

His knee stopped bouncing. Holmes didn't look at him. "That was an advance for the book."

Ryan shook his head. "It didn't come from your publisher. It came from a Genevieve Shaw. Who is she? Where can I find her?" His phone buzzed in his pocket. He glanced at the message. Cathleen had sent him the background checks on the two.

The man laughed. "I don't know who she is."

"Then why did she send you money if you don't know her?" He leaned close. "We know you recorded over Mrs. Narvel naming the men who helped her husband finance the ski resort. Does Genevieve Shaw have anything to do with Vince Barsotti?"

The man squirmed in the chair. His legs moved as if he wanted to crawl up in the chair. "How should I know? I don't know who this Bar-Barsotti fellow is."

Just saying the name had the writer breaking out in a sweat. He didn't act like a man who had successfully blackmailed a crime boss. These were the actions of a man who had been threatened.

"Sit tight." Ryan left the room and headed straight to his laptop. He pulled up Cathleen's reports and things started to fall into place.

~*~

Shandra took Ryan's advice and didn't wait up for him. Not long after slipping into bed, Ella visited her.

"What are you showing me?" Shandra asked her grandmother.

Ella sat upon a cloud, her face pointed to the ground below. Shandra leaned to see what Grandmother watched. Two women were circling as if sizing one another up and deciding when to jump at the other.

"I don't understand."

Grandmother pointed her crooked finger. A child played not far from the two. She couldn't discern who the child might be. Boy or girl.

She stared and the child and women disappeared like steam.

The bedroom door closing jarred her from her sleep. Shandra sat up and turned the light on. Ryan stood by the closet, unbuttoning his shirt. She picked up the paper she'd written the names on.

"I have the names of Mrs. Narvel's cousin and her husband. I feel like they might help us find her killer."

Ryan sat on the bed and pulled off his boots.

"The last name is Shaw."

"It was before she married Dwight Grun." She rubbed his shoulders. "How do you know that?"

"Cathleen did background checks on Mr. Holmes and Miss Tapfer."

She sucked in her breath. "She really is related to Mrs. Narvel?"

"Yes, Miss Tapfer is my victim's cousin." He sighed and relaxed as she continued to massage his shoulders and neck.

"Why did she pretend to be her granddaughter? And how bizarre that Jeffrey Holmes, the writer helping Mrs. Narvel with her memoirs, would know her cousin."

"It was Miss Tapfer's idea. She sent a letter to Mrs. Narvel pretending to be someone from the Portland Historical Society suggesting Mr. Holmes and asking for a memoir to put in the section of the museum with her family's memorabilia." Ryan finished undressing and getting ready for bed as Shandra digested the information.

When he returned to the room, she had to ask, "Why did she present herself as the granddaughter rather than who she really is?"

"According to Miss Tapfer, her grandmother was cut off from all the family money when she married the convict. When Holmes told her about the baby given up for adoption, Miss Tapfer went to work digging up family information and faking the birth certificate. She even paid Holmes to be part of the scheme using her grandmother's maiden name, Shaw."

Shandra reclined onto the pillows. "But did either confess to killing Mrs. Narvel?"

"No. But they both are still hiding more. I have them in the Huckleberry Jail until tomorrow morning. It was too late tonight to talk to Dr. Porter and see if he wanted to press charges for the forgery." Ryan slid into bed. He wrapped his arms around her. "I've been thinking of this the last three hours."

She sighed and snuggled close. Closing her eyes, Ella appeared, jogging her memory. "Right before you walked in I had a dream."

"Your grandmother?"

"Yes. Two women were circling like they were fighting and a child sat off to the side playing."

"That's it?"

"Yes."

He kissed her neck. "I'm too tired to think. We'll discuss it in the morning."

"Okay." She remained in his arms, her mind flipping through what they knew about so far. Was the child, Dr. Porter, Miss Tapfer, or the child Mrs. Narvel lost?

~*~

In the morning, Ryan's first call was to Dr. Porter. He couldn't keep Holmes and Tapfer locked up much longer without charges. He was still at Shandra's when he called.

"Detective Greer, have you found out who killed my aunt?" Dr. Porter asked when Ryan identified himself.

"Not yet. I have some other family issues I

need to discuss with you. Will you still be home in an hour?"

"I can be, but what family issues?" There as a pause. "It's that Tapfer woman, isn't it?"

"I'd like to discuss it in person. I'll be there in forty-five minutes." Ryan moved to push the off button when he heard Miranda say, "Bring Shandra with you."

He grinned. It appeared the vivacious young woman wasn't letting Dr. Porter push her away.

"Get dressed," he said to Shandra who stood in the kitchen, eating a piece of toast.

"Why?" She headed out of the room before he could answer.

Ryan's gaze followed her departure. The short shorts and skimpy tank top she wore to bed didn't look sexy when he folded them, but on her body, they looked like hundred-dollar lingerie.

To make sure she hurried, he gathered up his computer and stood by the door. Sheba woofed. He opened the door, wondering how the dog knew he was standing by the front door and not the back.

Shandra stepped out of the bedroom ten minutes after he'd told her to get dressed and she looked as attractive as most women looked after hours in front of a mirror.

"Where are we going?" she asked, slinging her leather fringed bag over her shoulder.

"To talk with Dr. Porter. Miranda asked that I bring you." He opened the door. Sheba bounded out in front of them.

"Should I take my Jeep?" She dug in her purse.

"Yes. You'll want to come home long before I'll be ready." He stepped close as her face glowed with triumph and her hand appeared with the keys. "See you at Doc Porter's." He kissed her full on the lips and headed to his SUV.

He glanced in the rearview mirror as he headed down her road. Shandra was already nosing her copper-colored Jeep out of the barn.

She remained right behind him all the way to town and out the other side. He pulled up into the driveway at the Victorian house and noticed Miranda's car and Dr. Porter's, side-by-side in the open garage. Either she came over early that morning or they were already living together.

He waited for Shandra to meet him at the walkway. She nodded toward the garage and grinned. "It looks like Miranda isn't losing any time."

"Yes."

He rapped with the knocker.

Mrs. Alvarez opened the door. "Come in. Dr. Porter and the miss are waiting in the parlor."

Shandra entered ahead of him. Ryan followed, but kept his eye on the housekeeper. She walked down the hall and disappeared at the stairway.

He still wondered if Dana Alvarez had anything to do with the older woman's death. She'd more or less pointed her finger at the writer, but that could have been to move his suspicions from her.

"Good morning," Shandra said, hugging Miranda and Dr. Porter.

Ryan shook hands with Dr. Porter. Miranda

motioned for Ryan and Shandra to sit on the chairs in front of the couch where she and Dr. Porter sat.

"What is this all about?" Dr. Porter asked.

Ryan told them about Miss Tapfer being a cousin and about the scheme she and Mr. Holmes had planned to play on his aunt.

"Why would she want to scam her family? All she had to do was talk to my aunt and she would have been generous." Dr. Porter stared at Ryan as if looking for an explanation.

He couldn't help the man. It didn't make sense to him either.

Mrs. Alvarez appeared in the doorway with a wheeled cart loaded with coffee and pastries. She rolled the cart over to Miranda.

"How did you get that cart up the stairs?" Shandra asked.

"The cart stays in the closet at the end of the hall. The food comes up a dumb waiter near that closet." Mrs. Alvarez faced Dr. Porter. "Is this all?"

"Yes. Thank you." Dr. Porter fingered a filled pastry, putting it on a plate. "Do you think my filing charges against the two will help solve my aunt's death?"

Mrs. Alvarez stopped at the door as if to listen.

Ryan put that away to speculate on at a later date. "No. What I want from them is the complete truth. I was hoping you would reach out to Miss Tapfer as family and see if you couldn't learn more about her circumstances and why she would go to such lengths to get a piece of the family money." He smiled at Miranda. "Perhaps you could invite

Miss Tapfer and Mr. Holmes for dinner and charm them."

"That's not a bad idea," Miranda said, handing Ryan a cup of coffee.

Shandra jumped in with what she'd discovered. "I talked with Miranda's mom and discovered some things about the Porter family and Miss Tapfer's grandmother. I then looked through the old newspapers and put a few things together." She knew Ryan wasn't going to like her digging, but she couldn't help herself. She was now fully engaged in discovering the family dynamics.

"What did you discover?" Dr. Porter asked.

"That your aunt was at her cousin's wedding. She appeared to be the only Porter who attended, but then Mabel was Gladys' cousin on her mother's side, not the Porter side." Shandra had everyone's attention. "I was thinking if she attended the wedding, they may have stayed in contact. Is there a chance your aunt kept letters? And if she did, would you mind if I looked through them to see if she did correspond with Mabel?"

Dr. Porter thought on it for several moments. "Yes. I believe I did see a box of letters in her closet." He put a hand on Miranda's knee. "Why don't you and Shandra see if you can find them?"

Shandra's heart raced with anticipation. He was allowing her to go through his aunt's letters. She hoped the missives would explain the dream she had the night before.

Ryan stood when she shot to her feet. He captured her hand. "I'll be gone when you come back down. Call and we'll meet for lunch."

She nodded. He kissed her cheek and sat back down.

As Miranda led her out of the room, Shandra glanced over her shoulder at Ryan. Why had he made a point of everyone knowing he was leaving soon?

Chapter Nineteen

Ryan asked Dr. Porter a few more questions about his family before taking his leave. He could tell Shandra was curious about his production over being gone when she came down. A grin tipped his lips as he walked to his vehicle. She knew him too well.

He started up his SUV, backed out of the drive, and headed toward town. Once he was out of sight of the house, he made a U turn and parked. The house wasn't visible from here. He exited his vehicle and made his way to the back of the Narvel, or now, Porter residence. The house set by itself on a small hill. Lucky for him there were plenty of trees and bushes to shield his approach.

Mrs. Alvarez had been nervous every time he saw her. What or who was she hiding? He had a good idea it was her daughter. While waiting behind a tree and watching the back of the house, he dialed Dr. Porter's number. Best to discover if the girl was now welcome or not before he confronted her.

"Hello," Dr. Porter answered.

Ryan could hear Miranda and Shandra talking in the background.

"This is Detective Greer. I forgot to ask if you are allowing Dana Alvarez to live in the basement with her mother?"

There was the sound of the doctor exhaling. "I feel for Mrs. Alvarez, having lost a friend in my aunt, but at the same time after Dana stole that necklace, and the only person here all day is her mother, I asked that she not stay in the house. Is she here?"

"I'm not sure. I wanted to make sure you had asked her to leave before I confronted her. Thank you." He heard Shandra chuckle. "Are the ladies making any progress in finding the letters?"

"Yes, they are giggling over my uncle's letters to my aunt." The doctor sounded bemused by their light-heartedness.

Perhaps, Miranda and Shandra were the best people to help the doctor through his grief.

"I'll keep you up to date on what I learn." He closed the connection. Ten minutes later, he spotted Dana walking along the side of the house as if she didn't want anyone to see her. He waited for her to get to the end of the driveway before showing himself and walking up to her.

"Ms. Alvarez, Dr. Porter told me you aren't welcome at his home. Why are you sneaking out of the back door?" He fell into step beside the young woman.

She stared at her feet and kept walking.

"Nothing to say?" Ryan noted she was walking toward the resort and not town. "Why are you headed toward the lodge?"

"I have a job. You're keeping me from getting there on time."

He waved back the way they'd come. "If you want to walk with me to my vehicle, I'll give you a ride to the resort."

She glanced over at him. "This a trick?"

He stopped. "A trick? No. I'm offering to give you a ride to work. I do have some questions for you."

Dana pivoted, heading back the way they'd walked. "Will they make me late for work?"

She was sure conscientious about work all of a sudden.

"No. I won't make you late for work." He picked up his stride and she jogged along beside him. When they were in the SUV, he drove toward the lodge. "What is your job at the lodge?"

"I clean rooms." She'd shoved her hands in the pocket of her hoodie. "You said you had other questions for me."

"Yes. When you were stealing the necklace and any other time you were upstairs, where you were trespassing, did you hear any other conversations?"

He glanced over as she peered at him from the shadow of the hood.

"You want me to tell you everything I heard?"

"Yes."

"Even if it was an argument between Alex and his aunt?" Her tone revealed she thought he was on the doctor's side.

"Even an argument between Alex and his aunt. Everyone living in that house is a suspect."

She flinched. Was that a reaction to the fact she was the killer?

"He and Gladys were arguing pretty good a couple nights before she died."

"What about?" Dr. Porter hadn't mentioned this.

"He told his aunt he was going to ask someone to marry him. She told him he was being selfish putting his genetic disorder onto another male child if he didn't find the cure. He said he was tired of being alone and had found someone who helped him enjoy life." She waved a hand. "He does lead a pretty boring life. He sleeps, works as a doctor and works on a cure. That is about it."

Ryan agreed. "How angry did they both get? Did he ever mention who the woman was?"

She looked at him as if his head had just spun like a top. "The lady staying in the house now. Miranda."

"She moved in?" They'd just announced the engagement and she was already living there? He didn't want to think Miranda could have had anything to do with the old woman's fall.

"Yeah, the night they announced their engagement she stayed and was packing in suitcases and boxes the next morning."

"What did Mrs. Narvel say when she learned who the woman was the doctor wanted to marry?"

"She stopped hollering. I think she said something like, she is a delightful girl. But could become a young widow."

Ryan had the feeling that while Mrs. Narvel had funded her nephew's research, she hadn't had a lot of faith in him. He pulled up to the front of the lodge. "Here you go. I hope I got you here on time."

She opened the door and hopped out. The slam of the door was the only thank you he received.

~*~

Shandra sat at the desk in the room that had been Mrs. Narvel's. Miranda stood on a chair, pulling another flowered box down off the highest shelf in the closet.

"I can't believe she saved every letter she ever received." Miranda sat the box on the end of the desk.

"The last box appeared to be letters she'd received from Alex." Shandra felt funny calling Dr. Porter by his given name, but Miranda had insisted when Shandra had mentioned him by his occupation.

"Then we've uncovered letters from her husband and Alex. Maybe this box is from other relatives." Miranda pulled the lid off with a flourish.

Shandra pulled out the first letter and stared at the return address. *Portland. Mabel Shaw.* "We found it!" she said, and opened the envelope.

She scanned the information. It appeared to be a casual dispensing of information between cousins.

"Let's put them in order by postmarks."

They each grabbed a handful and began sorting them onto the bed in chronological order.

Alex walked back in when they were sorting the last handful. "Did you find what you were looking for?"

"I'm not sure. But these are all letters from Mrs. Narvel's cousin, Mabel. Miss Tapfer's grandmother." Shandra picked up one dated a month before the Shaw-Grun wedding. Mabel was begging her cousin to come to the wedding. "*I won't have any other relatives. Please, if you love me as you say you do, you won't let our mother's differences keep you away.*"

"We need to start at the beginning of these. Somewhere we have to find out what caused Mabel and Gladys' mothers to be on the outs." She replaced the letter asking Gladys to come to the wedding and picked up the second one.

"I need to get to work," Alex said, putting a hand on Miranda's shoulder.

She stood and walked him to the bedroom door.

Shandra ignored their good-bye as she read the letter and gained more insight into the two women. They appeared as close as sisters in some letters, yet the family squabble wasn't mentioned. She'd read all the way up to the wedding letter, when Miranda returned, carrying a tray with coffee and cookies.

"I thought you could use a break," she said, placing the tray on the desk.

"Thanks." Shandra set the letter she'd been reading down and walked over to the desk. She picked up a cup of steaming coffee and smiled at her friend. "You're making yourself right at home."

Miranda blushed. "Mother thinks I'm moving too fast. But if we only have fifteen years together, I don't want to wait around to see if Alex finds a cure. He says he's getting close." She closed her eyes for a few seconds and took a deep breath. "I can't think he won't succeed."

Shandra understood. Even though Ryan's job put him in danger every day, she couldn't dwell on it. She had to look forward to their time together and not fear what could happen.

"How are you getting along with Mrs. Alvarez? I assume you'll keep her on since your parents aren't going to let you leave the restaurant." Shandra sipped her coffee.

Miranda was slow replying. "Mrs. Alvarez is a bit pushy. When I said something to Alex, he said I must be mistaken. Perhaps she was still just upset over his aunt or we didn't understand one another." She shook her head. "I asked if I could come to the kitchen and see what was in the pantry. I like to cook and would like to make some meals for Alex. She told me my place was above the basement."

Shandra remembered how surprised the housekeeper and her daughter had been when she showed up in the kitchen looking for a garbage bag. "She is protective of her space, I guess."

"And her daughter. I could tell she wasn't happy when Alex told Mrs. Alvarez her daughter could not be trusted and could not stay, even in the basement." Miranda picked up a sugar cookie, nibbling on it.

"That's understandable. Look at how easy it was for her to steal a necklace. Did Alex tell you anything about the daughter?" The vision of the woman lurking at the corner of the house the day of the murder came back to her.

"She dropped out of school but had been a good student." Miranda scrunched her face. "Why would a good student drop out of school?"

Shandra shook her head. Most people who were good students went on to college or a job with a career.

"He said she'd moved to Spokane and was working there before she moved back to Huckleberry. When she first came back, she had an apartment. But about a month ago, she moved in with her mother in the basement." Miranda waved at the letters on the bed. "We need to read the rest of these so I can get to work."

Shandra put down her cup and resumed reading the letters. They mentioned Mabel's, at first, emphatic pleas for Gladys to help her husband, but later, she said she was moving to Las Vegas to find work for her and her daughter, Genevieve. After that the letters only came at Christmas time with only a few brief sentences about everything being good. The letters stopped about the time Mr. Narvel started building the ski resort.

Miranda went to get ready for work while Shandra stacked the letters back in the box in order. Miss Tapfer might like the letters. They gave a small glimpse into her grandmother's life. The box of letters from Mr. Narvel to Gladys still sat on the bedside table. She and Miranda had read a few, but when she'd discovered all the letters were between the married couple, she'd moved on, looking for the letters from Mabel. But could there have been mention of Vince Barsotti in the letters?

Miranda returned to the room. She wore a fancy dress and high heels.

"You're ready for work. I'll take off." Shandra eyed the married couple's box of letters. "Do you think Alex would mind if I took this box of letters? I'll bring them back tomorrow."

Miranda shrugged. "I don't see why he'd care. He'll probably toss them when we remodel the room."

Shandra tucked the box under her arm and followed her friend down the stairs. It was two. Maybe Ryan would be up for a late lunch. With the box tucked into the back of the Jeep so Sheba couldn't scatter the letters, she drove to the Huckleberry Police Station. She started to get out of her vehicle when Mr. Holmes and Miss Tapfer stomped out of the building. They had a heated conversation and both went their separate ways.

Chapter Twenty

Ryan stood inside the Huckleberry P.D. watching the writer and Dr. Porter's cousin arguing. He had no doubt they were bickering over who said too much. They were lucky Dr. Porter hadn't pressed charges. Unfortunately for them, they were still his best suspects in the murder of Mrs. Narvel.

The two parted, stomping in opposite directions.

A flash of light drew his attention to a parked vehicle. Shandra's Jeep. He left the police station, meeting Shandra on the sidewalk. "Are you just now finishing your letter hunt?"

"Yes. Care to join me for a late lunch?" She glanced back at the Jeep. "That is if you don't mind grabbing something and going where Sheba can have a romp. She's been stuck in the Jeep all morning."

He pulled out his phone and hit the speed dial for Ruthie's. "Hi Ruthie, this is Ryan. Can I get my usual and Shandra's usual to go? We'll be by shortly to pick it up."

"I'll have it ready." Ruthie hung up.

"There you go. We'll get Sheba and walk to Ruthie's then on over to the park behind the Catholic Church." They didn't get many chances to act like a normal dating couple, even though they lived together. He liked the idea of a picnic.

"That is a wonderful idea." She fairly skipped back to her Jeep and snapped a leash on her bear-sized dog.

Sheba leaped out and hurried over to sniff him and wag her tail.

"How's it going? You ready for a walk?" he asked the animal. She wagged her tail harder and her tongue drooped out of her mouth.

"It's a yes," Shandra said, grasping his hand. The three of them strolled down to the end of the block and turned right. Another block and they were on Huckleberry Street, getting ready to cross to the café.

"Isn't that Mr. Holmes?" Shandra asked, pointing with the hand holding the leash.

Ryan followed her arm and was surprised to see the writer and Dr. Porter meeting. Could the two of them have been working together? "Let's go right here a minute." They continued down the opposite side of the street.

The meeting was more of a confrontation. Holmes voice carried across the street. "I don't care if you don't believe me. I want paid for what I have created of your aunt's memoir."

Dr. Porter's reply was too low for him to hear.

"Listen here. I gave up another job and a novel to do this story, you aren't going to stiff me." The writer stabbed a finger into Dr. Porter's chest. The doctor took a step back, grabbed the man's arm, and spun him, holding the other man's arm behind his back much like an apprehension hold.

"After what you did, trying to pass someone off as my aunt's granddaughter, I can't believe you have the gall to ask me to pay you for work you didn't finish."

"You want me to finish the book? I can, right down to telling who the murderer is."

Dr. Porter shoved the man away from him. "What are you talking about?"

Holmes had a smug grin on his face, much like the one he'd had when he said he knew more about Dr. Porter's aunt than her nephew did. "I saw you driving toward the house when I was headed to pick up Genie. You were at the house at the time of your aunt's unfortunate fall."

Ryan didn't think the doctor's face could go any paler, but it did. "What are you talking about?"

"I'm saying. You had more motive than anyone to want your aunt dead. And I saw you headed that way that morning." Holmes walked up close to the doctor.

His voice was too low to hear. By the doctor's reaction, the writer was blackmailing him.

"I won't pay you a dime and you can tell

whoever you want you saw me driving toward my aunt's house. That doesn't prove I was there, because I wasn't." Dr. Porter pivoted and strode down the sidewalk. A car half a block away chirped and the lights flashed. He slid into the car seconds before the engine roared to life and he turned the corner, apparently heading for the clinic.

Shandra tugged on his hand. "Should you go talk to Mr. Holmes or even Dr. Porter?"

"No. I owe you lunch. Come on." He led her across the street. The writer had headed down a side street when he caught a glimpse of them.

At Ruthie's Shandra stood outside holding her dog, while he went in to get their order. Miss Tapfer sat in a booth by herself. She was stirring a straw in a chocolate milk shake, her gaze on the motion.

"A penny for your thoughts," he said.

She spun toward him a huge grin on her face, only to turn dark and sullen. "Are you going to follow me around since I didn't give you the answers you wanted?"

"No. I'm picking up my lunch and saw you sitting here lost in thought."

Ruthie walked over carrying a bag of burgers and fries and the two drinks. "It's about time you and Shandra slowed down. How's she feeling? Her cold getting better?"

"She is feeling much better. We're going on a picnic." Ryan smiled and paid the owner of the café.

Miss Tapfer made a disgusted sound and slurped her shake.

Ruthie rolled her eyes and waved at Shandra standing outside the glass door.

Ryan left the café and grasped Shandra's free hand. "Mind if we do a little surveillance?"

She smiled. "No. Who are we waiting for?"

He grinned and pulled her around the corner and down the alley that ran behind Ruthie's.

"Are we going to return to Ruthie's through the back door?" Her voice lifted an octave over her excitement.

"You shouldn't get excited over a stake out. You could be hurt and I'd never be able to live with myself." He pulled her close. "We're just going to ask Ruthie to let me know who meets with Miss Tapfer." He led her down the alley and up to the back door of the café.

Shandra handed the leash to Ryan. "I'll go in and make the request. Just in case Miss Tapfer might see you." She kissed his cheek before he could argue and walked into the short hall with the large freezer and pantry before stepping into the kitchen.

Ruthie was working up pie crust. "What are you doing back here? I thought you had a picnic to go to?" She wiped her hands and walked to where Shandra stood just at the edge of the kitchen.

"Ryan would like you to let him know who Miss Tapfer, the woman sitting by herself drinking a chocolate shake, is waiting for." She smiled. "It's police business."

Ruthie's chocolate drop eyes grew rounder. "Does he suspect her of killing Mrs. Narvel?"

"I don't know who he suspects. It seems to change every day." Shandra wasn't lying. The information he gathered each day had swung the proof against more than one person.

"I bet it's that writer. I don't like his smarmy smile or fake interest in things." Ruthie went back to the crust. "I'll call Ryan."

"Thanks." Shandra returned to the alley.

Ryan was sipping on his drink. "Will she call me?"

"Yes." Her stomach rumbled. "I'm starving. Let's go eat."

They walked to the small park. Shandra let Sheba off the leash. The big dog bounded across the ground, squatting on the far edge of the slowly greening grass.

Ryan's phone buzzed. He answered it and nodded.

"What was that?" she asked.

"One set of prints on the oxygen canister belonged to Mrs. Narvel. Hopefully, one or both of the other sets will be in the national system."

"Do you think you'll have this figured out before I leave for my show?" She hated the idea of leaving and not knowing what had happened. Especially, when Grandmother had been coming to her in dreams.

"I hope I do. We're still waiting on more information on both Holmes and Tapfer." Ryan handed her cheeseburger and caramel shake to her.

"What about the things Mr. Holmes accused Dr. Porter with? Being at his aunt's at the time of her death?" She drew the thick caramel ice cream up the straw and into her mouth. Nothing compared to Ruthie's caramel shakes.

"Part of it could have been Holmes trying to blackmail the doctor or trying to put blame on him. But as pale as Dr. Porter's face went, there is some truth in it." Ryan unwrapped his burger. "I'll have to question the doctor about it."

"I hope it's something innocent. Miranda is so happy. I'd hate to have her future husband be a murderer." Shandra shuddered. If Dr. Porter killed his aunt it would shake the whole community. He'd given medical attention to everyone at some point in the years he'd lived here.

"Did you find out anything from the letters?" Ryan asked.

"Not really. I could never discover what the feud between Mrs. Narvel's mother and her aunt was about. The bad blood was only mentioned once but not what it was." She chewed on a bite of her burger and swallowed. "I brought the box of letters from Mr. Narvel home with me. Miranda said she didn't think Alex would mind. I probably won't find anything, but I didn't get a chance to go through them." She remembered Miranda's comment about Mrs. Alvarez. "What is your professional opinion of Mrs. Alvarez?"

"The housekeeper? She's nervous and nosey. But she seems to keep all she sees and hears to herself."

"Would you consider her pushy?" She used Miranda's words for the woman.

"Pushy? No. She did get a bit flustered when she couldn't do a job she needed to that first day, but I wouldn't call her pushy." He studied her. "Why are you asking?"

"Miranda called her pushy. She wanted to see what was in the pantry and to cook for Alex and Mrs. Alvarez told her to stay above the basement."

Ryan nodded his head. "Her daughter is the only thing she might be pushy about. I caught Dana coming out of the basement this morning. She said she was on her way to work at the lodge. When I called Dr. Porter, he said she wasn't supposed to be living in the house. He couldn't trust her since she'd stolen the necklace."

Shandra sipped her shake and nodded her head. That made sense. A mother protecting her young. Images of the dream came to her. "Do you think Mrs. Alvarez got in a discussion with Mrs. Narvel about Dana and it ended up with the older lady falling down the stairs?" Before Miranda's comment, she hadn't thought the housekeeper brave enough to get in a confrontation.

"It's as good of an explanation as anything we've come up with. Or, Mrs. Alvarez didn't want Miranda in the basement because she'd see Dana was still living there. And the housekeeper could get fired for not following Dr. Porter's directions." Ryan held out a paper cup of sweet potato fries to her.

She took one and chewed. They weren't warm anymore. She loved the fries piping hot. Maybe Ryan would like sweet potato fries if they were luke warm.

Ryan's phone buzzed.

"Hi Ruthie." He listened. "I had a feeling. Thank you for calling." He shoved his phone back in the small holster on his belt.

"And who joined Miss Tapfer at the café?" Shandra didn't know who Ryan thought it would be.

"Mr. Jeffrey Holmes."

"No way! They were having a heated argument when I pulled up to the station." She replayed the scene she'd witnessed. She hadn't heard any words, but they had both looked angry.

"I believe that scene in front of the station was for my benefit. To make them look like they were blaming the other person. I bet, they'll be spending the night together in the fancy room they have at the lodge." Ryan wadded the paper from his burger and stuffed it into his empty fry cup. Then he shoved that into the bag. "You done?"

She tossed everything but the rest of her shake into the bag and called Sheba. Her big, furry friend ran back, her tongue hanging out and drool dangling from the corners of her mouth. Shandra laughed as Ryan backed away from the enthusiastic dog.

"Come here, girl." Shandra used her napkin to wipe the drool from Sheba's mouth.

"What are you going to do now?" Ryan asked, waiting for her to snap the leash on Sheba.

"Go home, start a list of what I need for my trip, and read the letters from Mr. Narvel to his wife." She grasped Ryan's outstretched hand and they walked by a garbage can where Ryan deposited the remains of their lunch.

Back at the police station, Ryan opened the Jeep door for both her dog and her. "Unless something comes up, I'll be home on time. I need more evidence to pull someone in for questioning." His gaze landed on the clinic across the street.

"You're going to ask Dr. Porter if he had returned to the house the morning of his aunt's death, aren't you?" They'd solved several murders together. She could tell that information had been banging around in his head.

"Yes, I am." Ryan kissed her and shut the door. "See you at home."

Shandra backed out of the parking space and watched Ryan walk across the street to the clinic. The doctor's car was in the parking lot. She drove out onto Huckleberry Street and sat at the stop sign trying to decide if she should go home or warn Miranda her fiancé might be a murderer.

Chapter Twenty-one

Ryan stepped into the clinic. The nose tingling, antiseptic scent and hushed sounds reminded him of his convalescence after the gang fight. No matter how long he lived, he would never be able to chase those memories and horrors from his mind. He shook off the thoughts and walked up to the receptionist.

"I'd like to talk with Dr. Porter, please." He flashed his badge even though he knew the young woman. He'd been here a couple of times to get reports on abuse and crash victims.

"He's with a patient. You'll have to wait." She pointed a pen toward a padded chair in the waiting area.

There was no one else in the room. "Will there be more patients coming in this afternoon?"

"No, he's with the last appointment. But the

doors will be open for another hour and someone could be a walk-in." She resumed typing on a keyboard.

He pulled out his phone and sent a text message to Cathleen, requesting a background check be done on Dr. Maynard Alexander Porter.

This afternoon, when the writer confronted him, the doctor had shown skill in defending himself. He would have never thought that of the man. Dr. Porter had always come across as bookish and non-aggressive.

Twenty minutes later, an elderly gentleman stepped into the waiting room from deeper in the building.

"Mr. Carmichael, would you like to book next month's check-up?" The receptionist was all smiles and friendliness with the patient.

"Yes, I would. It's easier to remember when I write it on the calendar and see it every day." The man took the card the woman handed him and tucked it in his wallet. "See you next month." He ambled to the outside doors and disappeared.

Ryan walked over to the reception desk as Dr. Porter entered the small office area carrying a file.

"Detective Greer, are you here for a medical appointment?" The man looked genuinely concerned.

"No. I have a couple more questions. Do you have an office?" Ryan waited as the man handed the young woman the file and waved him to come through the door to the rest of the building.

They walked in silence down the hall to a small

room with a desk, bookcases, and a diploma from Johns Hopkins Medical College with Dr. Porter's name written in a flourish.

Ryan took the chair in front of the desk.

"Have you learned any more about my aunt's death?" He paused and snapped his fingers. "Shandra found something in the letters."

"No, she hasn't so far. She did take home the letters from your uncle written to your aunt." Ryan leaned forward pulling out his notepad. "I've been easy on you, considering your grief and all, but I have some questions I need answers to."

Dr. Porter nodded his head. "I appreciate your consideration."

"Did you know that a mob boss named Vince Barsotti helped to finance Huckleberry ski resort and the growth of the town?"

"A mob boss? No, I thought Uncle Edward used family money."

"He used mob money. I've discovered that van loads of money came to the local bank and was laundered through the businesses here." Ryan flipped through his pages of notes.

"That was thirty years ago, what could that have to do with my aunt's death?" Dr. Porter tapped a pen on a desk calendar.

"Maybe nothing. But knowing the scam Mr. Holmes was playing with passing Miss Tapfer off as your aunt's granddaughter, I wouldn't put it past him, or both of them. He could have discovered this information and tried to blackmail either Mr. Barsotti's son or your aunt."

"Aunt Gladys would have told me and kicked Jeffery out if he had tried such a thing. She was proud of her place in this community." The doctor's skin was gaining a red hue as his anger grew.

"Are you sure Miss Tapfer hadn't been to the house before she arrived the day of the murder?" Ryan was tap dancing around what he really wanted to say. He hoped by catching the doctor off guard he'd slip up.

"I can't be positive. I work here five days a week and some evenings if there is an emergency. When I'm not here as the doctor on call, I'm either in the lab in the back or with Miranda. She could have visited before, but I'm sure if she had Aunt Gladys would have mentioned it. Or Mrs. Alvarez. She always answered the door for my aunt. Gladys thought it gave her more of an air or celebrity to have her housekeeper answer the door."

Ryan made a note to ask Mrs. Alvarez.

"I also have a witness who said you returned to the house the morning of your aunt's death."

The red coloring drained from the man's face. "Dana is still living at the house, isn't she?"

This caught Ryan by surprise. Dr. Porter thought it was Dana who fingered him. Always ready to improvise, he agreed. "Yes, I watched her leave by the back basement door this morning. We had a chat when I gave her a lift to work."

Dr. Porter leaned back in his chair and wiped a hand across his distraught face. "I want you to know, I did not kill my aunt. But I am guilty of theft."

Ryan didn't say anything. He'd learned keeping silent usually helped the guilty unburden faster than plying them with questions.

"I asked Dana to get my mother's wedding ring from my aunt's jewelry box. She knew how to get into the room and take jewelry. She'd proven it with the necklace she'd hocked." He stared at something over Ryan's right shoulder. "The ring was mine, but for some reason, my aunt felt she needed to have control over it. I had planned to ask Miranda to marry me that evening. But with what happened and my having asked Dana to steal the ring, I couldn't go through with it." His gaze landed on Ryan. "And I can vouch for Dana. She didn't hurt my aunt. While she was getting the ring, I was sitting in my car down the street talking to Aunt Gladys on the phone to keep her distracted. I hung up when I saw Dana walking toward my car." He covered his face with his hands. "I was ready to be happy with Miranda for whatever time I have left, but the whole thing has turned into one lie after another." He dropped his hands. "The only truth I know is I didn't kill Aunt Gladys and neither did Dana. I gave Miranda a new ring I purchased. I didn't want to taint our lives with the one stolen on the day of my aunt's death."

Ryan felt for the man, but at the same time, he had a job to do. "Do you think your aunt noticed the missing ring and confronted Dana later?"

"I doubt it. I gave Dana a cheap ring to slip into the little velvet bag the ring was kept in. Unless my aunt actually opened the little bag, she wouldn't have noticed the ring missing until she saw it on Miranda's finger the next day when I'd planned to announce our engagement."

He couldn't think of any other questions. Ryan stood. "Have you told Miranda all of this?"

The man shook his head.

"I've found it's best for a relationship to come clean about everything." Ryan left the office, walked down the hall, and out the front door. The man he'd left in the office looked as if he'd lost everything by telling the truth. It might clear him as a murder suspect. At least, once he talked to Dana and learned her side of the story. If she corroborated his story, they were off his suspect list. That still left four, possibly five more, if someone was blackmailing Barsotti.

~*~

Shandra sat in a booth at Rigatoni's. Miranda had let her in when she'd called and asked to speak with her. Mrs. Aducci had brought her an iced tea and told her daughter to sit and visit.

Miranda smiled watching her mother walk away. She turned her attention to Shandra and her smile slipped away. "We were together all morning. Has something come up about Alex's aunt's murder?"

"Yes, and no. I just want to make sure you really know the man you are going to marry." She'd thought she knew the man she'd fallen for in college only to find out he had a sadistic side to him.

"He's a good man. He saves lives, not takes

them. And he loved his aunt. When he talked about her you could feel how much he cared for her." She narrowed her eyes. "Did someone say something that has you suspecting him?"

"Ryan and I overheard something. The writer, Mr. Holmes, was threatening Alex on the street. He said he saw Alex heading to his aunt's house the day of the murder at about the time it happened."

She laughed. "He's a writer. He makes things up. He'd do anything to discredit Alex and get his girlfriend into the inheritance."

Shandra witnessed fear and spitefulness in Miranda. She'd never seen the woman anything other than jovial and gracious. "What do you know about Mr. Holmes and Miss Tapfer?"

"They were in here enough times I've overheard plenty of their conversations. They are always scheming how to get their hands on the Porter money."

"Porter? Shouldn't it be Narvel?" Did Dr. Porter have money they were after?

"No, Porter. The money that is funding Alex's research is Porter money. Money his aunt inherited at the deaths of her father and brother. He said she put it in a bank and invested. It was separate from what her husband used to set up the ski resort."

Shandra's brain was working overtime. "But Miss Tapfer is a Shaw, not a Porter. Do you know if the funds are to specifically go to a Porter heir?"

Miranda shrugged. "I don't know. Alex doesn't like to talk about money. He just says, when he comes up with a cure or even if he doesn't, there will be money to support me and any children we have."

"And Miss Tapfer wants a piece of it." A thought struck her. "You need to tell Alex to be careful. With Miss Tapfer as the last heir, even if she isn't a Porter, he could be in danger."

"Oh!" Miranda's eyes widened with fear. "I'm going to go call him right now." She left the booth and Shandra texted Ryan, asking him if he'd like to have dinner at the lodge.

They needed to learn more about the writer and the shirt-tail relative.

Chapter Twenty-two

Ryan pulled into the lodge parking lot and spotted Shandra's Jeep. Beyond the Jeep, in the trees along the west end of the parking lot, he saw Sheba bounding among the fir trees. He parked and headed across the parking lot. On his way, he noted both Holmes and Miss Tapfer's cars were in the lot.

He had a feeling those two were the reason Shandra had invited him to dinner at the lodge. Either she'd learned something new, or she was just curious how they were behaving after seeing their argument in front of the police station.

"Sheba needed to stretch her legs," Shandra said when he approached. The large dog was in pursuit of a squirrel circling a tree.

"I see that. Is there a reason you invited me to dinner here?" He kissed her cheek and watched the dog frolic like a puppy.

"I thought we might see what Mr. Homes and Miss Tapfer are doing." She called Sheba. The dog ran over, her tongue lolling out of her mouth as usual. At the Jeep, Shandra reached in, pulled out a bowl, and filled it with water from a half-full gallon jug. The dog noisily lapped the water.

"Miranda told me that the two have been in Rigatoni's talking about getting their hands on the Porter money. Turns out the money Dr. Porter uses for research is Porter money. Mrs. Narvel invested it and used it to educate and help her nephew. She didn't let her husband use a cent of it for the ski lodge." She picked up the empty bowl, and Sheba jumped in the vehicle. "Somehow Miss Tapfer knows about it and wants it." She closed the Jeep door.

Ryan grasped Shandra's hand, and they walked to the entrance of the lodge. "If it's Porter money, how can she get it? It looks like I need to have another discussion with the lawyer." He opened the door, waited for Shandra to walk through, and escorted her to the restaurant.

"Do you have reservations?" the hostess asked.

"No." Ryan motioned to the bar. "We can sit in the bar if you don't have any tables."

"We have tables, but you are welcome to order food in the bar."

Ryan led Shandra to the side door, leading into the bar. He had a feeling the two they were looking for would rather hide in the bar than in the more open restaurant area.

They took a table at the far corner where they

could sit facing the room and the door.

"Do you think they will come in here?" Shandra took the seat he held for her.

"If I've read them correctly." He sat and within minutes a waiter arrived to take their drink and dinner order. The waiter left and Ryan shifted his attention to Shandra.

"I was here the other day. Your friend Ms. Gamble helped me learn which room the two are staying in." Ryan scanned the bar. For early in the evening the place was filling quickly.

The waiter returned with their drinks.

Shandra picked up her iced tea and sipped. Ryan raised his glass and spotted Holmes. He entered talking to Sidney Doring.

"Do you see who he's talking with?" Shandra asked. Her derision for the man deepened her voice.

He'd locked Doring up for assaulting Shandra. And the man had been on his suspect list for two previous murders.

"I hope he doesn't see us," Shandra said, visibly shrinking in her seat.

"He can't do anything to us. We're customers here to have dinner." Ryan put a hand on her knee. "He can't hurt you. I won't let him." He peered into her eyes and saw the fire come back. Since learning of her abusive ex-lover, he wasn't about to let her become a victim to anyone again.

Doring shook hands with Holmes and walked out of the bar. Moments later, Miss Tapfer appeared. She went straight to Holmes' table. They kissed and sat down, facing the dance floor.

"We're too far away to hear anything," Shandra said, breaking into his thoughts.

"I see that. But we can watch them and see how they behave." He did a quick assessment of how much commotion they would make if they moved to a table closer to Holmes and Miss Tapfer. Their waiter arrived with salads. "Do you mind if we switch tables. That one over there looks like it might be cooler than this corner." Ryan held his hand out to Shandra. They both picked up their glasses and sat quickly and quietly at the table directly behind the writer and woman. Ryan made sure their backs were to the couple. If they happened to glance over their shoulders they would only see his and Shandra's backs.

The waiter placed their salads on the table and left. Shandra leaned into him and whispered, "You are a genius."

The admiration in her voice made him grin and kiss her lips. "Thanks. Now we have to hope they speak loud enough we can hear," he whispered back.

They both leaned back in their chairs and chewed their salads slowly.

"I don't think you can pin this on my cousin. He has to have an alibi. Just seeing him driving in the direction of the house doesn't mean he went there," Miss Tapfer said.

"Baby, if we can pin this on him, you are the only living heir. All that money has to come to you." Holmes voice rang with greed.

Ryan wondered if he even had feelings for the

woman. Though while questioning her, he'd noted she wasn't the innocent pushover she allowed Holmes to see. He had a feeling the writer was a pawn in the woman's scheme to get the money and the man thought she was his pawn.

"All my life I listened to my grandmother say her cousin had money and she hoped the feud would be forgotten and the money would come to me. She didn't expect Gladys to die before her nephew." Miss Tapfer knew about Dr. Porter's life expectancy. It didn't sound like she was willing to wait the twelve to fifteen years to see if the man died from his disease.

Shandra bumped Ryan's arm. "Did you hear that?" She couldn't believe how cold and callous the woman sounded. "I told Miranda to warn Dr. Porter to be careful. I don't think the two behind us want to wait much longer for the money."

"Me either. But we don't have enough proof to have an officer keep an eye on them."

The waiter brought their food and took away their empty salad plates.

"The old woman dying before you ingratiated yourself to her hadn't been expected. Now you'll have to make sure your cousin believes you want nothing more than to connect with family," Mr. Holmes said.

A phone rang behind them.

"Speak of the devil. It's your cousin." Mr. Holmes said. "Hello. You want to talk about me finishing the book?"

Shandra leaned back hoping to hear what Alex

was asking. Ryan put a hand on her leg as she pressed backwards and her front chair legs came off the floor.

"I know what the call is about," Ryan whispered in her ear.

She studied his face.

"You want Genie and I to come to dinner tomorrow night? Sure. I'll let her know."

There was a sound of clothing rustling.

"Well?" Genie asked him.

"You and I are invited to have dinner with your cousin and his fiancée tomorrow night at seven." Silverware clattered.

"His fiancée? When did that happen?" Genie asked, her voice tight and forced.

"I'm not sure but it's since your old aunt died. Kind of gives him another reason to want her dead, doesn't it?"

The insinuation in the man's voice sent a shiver down Shandra's spine. "He wants to pin this on Alex pretty bad. Almost to the point it would throw the police off of him," she whispered to Ryan.

He nodded and continued eating.

"Do you mean she was against him getting married?" Genie's excited voice proved she was interested in this tidbit.

"I happen to know the two argued about his getting married just days before your cousin took her fall."

Shandra narrowed her eyes at the man's smug comment. A thought came to her. She leaned close to Ryan. "Do you think he was listening into every conversation Mrs. Narvel had?"

"With his room across the hall from hers and the only landline upstairs in her room, he could have easily heard the phone ring and listened in on her conversations, as well as any in the house if he snuck around."

Shandra hadn't liked the writer from the beginning. She was liking him even less as she listened to him.

Dream a Little Dream jingled from her phone. She grabbed her purse and headed out the door, pulling her phone from the bag.

"Hello?"

"Shandra, it's Miranda."

"Hi. Is something wrong?" Her friend didn't sound her usual self.

"No, not really. Well, yes. Alex invited Jeffrey, the writer and Genie, his cousin, to dinner tomorrow night. I know it would be awkward to have Ryan here, considering he thinks they're suspects, but could you come? It will be an odd number of people, but I really think you should be here to kind of help me keep things civil."

"Of course, I'll come. If you want an even number, I can bring Lil or Ruthie. She might like a night away from the café." Shandra decided Ruthie would be a better person to bring. Lil had a hard time hiding her feelings if she didn't like someone.

"Would you? Oh, thank you! I just didn't think I could play referee all night."

"Not a problem. That's what friends are for. I'll see you at seven."

There was an awkward pause. "Um, I didn't tell you what time," Miranda said.

"That's when most people have dinner parties, isn't it?" Shandra slapped her hand to her forehead.

"Yeah, seven. Okay. See you then."

Shandra ended the call as Ryan walked out of the restaurant. "Did you learn anything else?"

"No, they're speculating on why Dr. Porter wants them to come to dinner." He pointed to her phone. "Anyone important?"

"Miranda. I've been invited to the dinner tomorrow night. Without you. She thinks it would be awkward if you were there." Shandra put a hand on his chest, hoping he didn't put up a fight.

"I'll be outside." He smiled.

She studied him a minute then grinned. "You asked Alex to set the dinner up, didn't you?"

"Yes. I just didn't expect you to be there." He grasped her hand. "Let's go home."

"I have to stop by Ruthie's. I told Miranda I'd bring a date." She wiggled her eyebrows.

Ryan laughed. "You're taking Ruthie as your plus one?"

"It was her, Lil, or Naomi." She ticked of the names of the only women she felt comfortable enough around to have them sit in on a dinner party that could turn into something interesting. None of those three would ever say anything to anyone else if things went wrong.

"I think Ruthie is a good choice. Lil would scowl at everyone the whole night and Naomi is too soft. If the conversation got heated she'd be under the table." Ryan led her over to her Jeep. "I'll follow you."

She faced him. "You don't have to follow me home. I've driven that road more times than you and haven't had any problems."

"Humor me. I'm following you." He kissed the tip of her nose and pivoted, striding across the lot to his SUV.

~*~

Shandra stopped in front of the café. A high school girl slapped a rag across a table, Maxwell, Ruthie's fiancé, danced about the restaurant with a mop that came to his belly button. The big man should have been a pro football player instead of a mortician.

"Shandra, what are you doing here so late?" Maxwell asked, dropping the mop in an industrial mop bucket.

"I was going to ask Ruthie for a favor. She around?"

He shook his head. "She was beat. I told her to take a bath and go to bed."

"I'd like her to be my plus-one at a dinner tomorrow night at Dr. Porter's. Could you have her give me a call in the morning to let me know if she can make it?"

He shook his head. "I can already tell you she won't be there. She has a catering gig. The Catholic Church fundraiser." He snapped his fingers. "I can go. That is if your boyfriend don't mind." Maxwell gave her an exaggerated wink.

She hadn't thought about bringing a man, but

Maxwell would be good. If the doctor and writer came to fisticuffs he could break them up in a heartbeat. She held out a hand. "It's a date. I'll be by to get you about six-thirty. That is if you don't need to help Ruthie."

"She don't like me helping with the catering. She says it gives people the jeebees having a mortician serve them salad." He laughed and grabbed the mop. "See you tomorrow night."

Shandra laughed and returned to her Jeep. Ryan sat in his vehicle talking on the phone. She started up the Jeep and pulled onto the street and he was right behind her. There was a time when his protectiveness would have made her mad. Now she understood he did it because he cared about her.

~*~

Ryan passed Shandra a mile from her driveway. He hurried up to the barn, parked, and had the barn doors open when she drove up. It was a small thing, but he liked doing little things for her.

Lil had left lights on in the house. They walked into a homey atmosphere. He had to admit, he felt more at home here than he did the home he grew up in.

"Did Ruthie agree to be your date?" he asked.

"I didn't get to talk to her. Maxwell said she had a rough day and was in bed already. He also said she had a catering job tomorrow night."

"What are you going to do?" He faced her and wondered what was up. Her eyes were shining with good humor and her lips were quirked in a silly smile.

"Maxwell agreed to be my date."

"Treat?" The more he thought about it, there wasn't anyone else he'd want in a house with a murderer protecting Shandra. "That's a good idea. Does he know we suspect Holmes and the cousin?"

"No. Should I fill him in when I pick him up?"

Ryan went to the fridge and pulled out a beer for him and a bottle of wine. "Let me think on it a bit. I'm not sure if he'd be more help if he didn't know anything or if he did." He poured a glass of wine for Shandra and handed it to her. "I wish I could be a fly on the wall tomorrow night."

She grinned. "I can't wait."

Chapter Twenty-three

Shandra rolled up to the back of Ruthie's café and Maxwell stepped out the back door, dressed in a button-up lavender shirt and dark gray slacks.

"Wow, you clean up nice!" she said, as he folded himself into the passenger seat of the Jeep.

He gave her a big white-toothed grin. "That's what my baby tells me all the time." He glanced over his shoulders as if worried someone might see him. "Don't tell her I wore her favorite shirt to dinner tonight." He laughed and shrugged. "It was the only clean one I had."

Shandra laughed, already enjoying her choice of plus-one. Ryan had decided it would be best to fill Maxwell in on what was happening. So, she did. Every last detail she knew about.

Maxwell whistled. "What have you dragged me into? I'm glad I'm here and not my sweet Ruthie."

He scowled at her. "I can't believe you were going to bring her along."

"We have nothing to worry about. No one is going to do anything with a house full of people. I think that's why Miranda invited me and a guest. The more people, the less likely things will become dangerous."

He scoffed. "Easy for you to say. You've been in tight scrapes more times than I have."

She agreed, but she also didn't feel they would be in any danger. Dr. Porter might, but she and Maxwell wouldn't.

A third car sat in the drive. It appeared the other guests were early. She parked behind the other car and put a hand on Maxwell's arm. "Remember, act natural. You can't go in there glaring or questioning people."

"I know. I can be cool and watch our backs at the same time." He stepped out of her Jeep and waited for her to catch up to him at the porch steps.

She passed him and grasped the knocker, giving it three smart raps.

Mrs. Alvarez answered the door. Her eyes widened in surprise at the sight of Maxwell.

"Hi," Shandra said. "This is my plus-one."

"They are in the parlor," Mrs. Alvarez said, stepping out of the way.

Shandra motioned for Maxwell to follow as she entered the parlor.

"Shandra, I'm so glad you could make it." Miranda rushed across the room, hugging her. She stepped back and held out her hand to Maxwell.

"You must be Shandra's guest. It's good to see you Maxwell."

The age difference in the two would have put them years apart in school but in this small community everyone knew everyone else.

"Maxwell, I'm surprised to see you without Ruthie. You could have brought her as well," Alex said, shaking hands.

"She had a fundraiser at the church to cater." He narrowed his eyes at Shandra. "Ruthie was Shandra's first choice."

"Yes, that's true. I asked Ruthie, and when she couldn't come, Maxwell was nice enough to step in." Shandra walked farther into the room, taking a seat on the small settee.

"How about a drink?" Alex asked.

Maxwell followed him over to the bar.

"Shandra, this is Jeffrey Holmes, the writer who was working on Mrs. Narvel's memoir, and this is Genie Tapfer. She claims to be Alex's cousin." Miranda didn't hide the animosity she felt toward the woman.

"Pleased to meet you." Shandra stood and shook hands with the pair.

"Are you Shandra Higheagle, the famous potter?" Jeffrey asked.

"I'm a potter, but I don't know how famous." She didn't like the way the man's face lit up.

"I've seen you with Detective Ryan," Genie said, bluntly and with a pointed stare.

"Yes, Detective Ryan and I are living together," Shandra said. She wouldn't deny it, they could ask anyone in town.

"Are you here spying on us?" the woman asked.

"No. Miranda is my friend, and she invited me to dinner." Shandra could see the woman would be tight-lipped and closed from her comment.

Maxwell brought Shandra a glass of wine. The only spots to sit were on the settee with her or on the couch with Alex and Miranda. Jeffrey and Genie had taken the two single chairs.

"Here Maxwell, you can share the couch with Alex, it's better suited for the two of you and I'll sit with Shandra." Miranda switched places.

Maxwell gave her a big smile, while sitting on the couch.

As she'd thought earlier, Miranda would make an excellent hostess for any party Dr. Porter wished to throw. Shandra sipped her wine and wondered at the awkward silence. Was this how it had been before they arrived? Or had they been discussing things no one wished guests to hear? Not one to waste time, she dove in with a question for Jeffery. "How is the book going?"

He threw a glare toward Alex and said, "It's stalled. I haven't been paid, and I refuse to continue until I am."

"I thought you didn't get paid until a book is published," Maxwell said, jumping into the conversation.

"Well, that's true when a writer writes a book that hasn't been contracted. But as a ghost writer-writing a book for someone else, I get paid before and during the writing." If the man had been a bird he would have preened his feathers.

"I see." Shandra leaned forward. "Who paid you before you started?"

The man's gaze darted to Genie before he focused on Shandra. "The Oregon Historical Society."

Shandra sipped her wine. Genie Tapfer had pretended to be the historical society. Which meant the writer was under contract to the estranged cousin. Not wanting them to realize she knew the truth, she asked, "Then wouldn't they be the ones to make your next payment?"

Jeffrey sputtered and Genie narrowed her eyes at Shandra.

"I like this house," Maxwell said, changing the topic. "Will you keep it?" he asked Alex.

Dr. Porter smiled at his fiancée. "Miranda says she loves the house. So, it looks like we'll keep it."

"Yes. The history, the way the rooms are laid out." She leaned closer to Shandra. "I just wish the kitchen was on this level so I could have made dinner instead of Mrs. Alvarez."

Food, cooking, and serving were in Miranda's bones. Shandra understood her friend's reluctance to leave a meal up to the housekeeper. She wanted to say, they could get rid of Mrs. Alvarez, but the last person to say that ended up dead. As the comment echoed in her mind, Shandra felt an epiphany.

"Oh my. I forgot to tell Ryan something about Sheba's food." Shandra pulled her phone from her purse as she stood. "I'll step out so I don't disrupt the conversation."

Maxwell and Miranda gave her inquisitive looks, the other three were caught in a staring match.

She stepped across the hall, making sure the housekeeper wasn't in the dining room before standing by the front door and dialing Ryan.

"Shandra, what are you doing calling? Is something wrong?"

"No. I know who did it." Shandra whispered into the phone.

"Who?"

"Mrs. Alvarez."

"The housekeeper? Why?"

"Mrs. Narvel wanted her daughter out of the house and she threatened to fire Mrs. Alvarez over the daughter." This was the reason. They could have quarreled over Dana and one push from Mrs. Alvarez and her problems were gone. Dr. Porter had a soft spot for the girl.

"We don't have proof. You didn't suggest that to anyone else, did you?" His concern for her dropped his voice lower.

"No. It just came to me as we were talking. Boy, is Genie Tapfer a witch. She clammed up after revealing she knew you and I are an item."

"Be careful. Did you clue Maxwell in?"

"Yes. I have to go. This is way too long of a conversation to tell you how to feed Sheba."

Ryan stared at the disconnected phone. "How to feed Sheba?" He huffed a laugh and shifted his attention back to the Victorian house. He sat in the trees about halfway between the front and back of the house. He wanted to see if anyone went in or out either door and he could see people through the dining room windows when they went in to eat.

He leaned against the tree and ran Shandra's idea through what he knew about the facts of the case. The housekeeper found the body and called 9-1-1. She was alone in the house with the victim, according to the others involved in the case. Dana was meeting Dr. Porter with the stolen ring. He confirmed he was still on the phone with his aunt when Dana was back in his sight. Those two had an illegal alibi, but an alibi. Holmes and Tapfer say they were together. But he had yet to find someone who could corroborate that. Mrs. Alvarez would do anything to keep her only child out of jail. But did she really believe Mrs. Narvel would fire her? She needed a place for both she and Dana to live. If Mrs. Narvel, the pinnacle of the Huckleberry society, fired her it was safe to say she wouldn't be able to find work in Huckleberry.

He liked the idea of the housekeeper for the murder. Shadows moved inside the dining room windows. Porter's guests were entering the dining room for the meal. Ryan pulled out a small pair of binoculars and studied the seating arrangement that he could see. Dr. Porter and Miranda were seated at the ends of the table. Maxwell's wide shoulders and back blocked whoever sat across from him. He couldn't see who sat next to him or who was across from that person. They were blocked by the wall between the two windows.

He switched his binoculars to infrared and searched the area behind the house. Movement caught his attention. He stayed inside the line of trees, moving to the back of the house. Dana stood by the basement door, handing items to three men.

He rushed out of the trees, gun raised. "Police Freeze!"

Dana ran into the house; the men took off through the back yard. Ryan raced after the men, jumping over the items they dropped in his path. All three leaped over the fence in the back.

"Go!" someone shouted.

An engine revved and tires squealed.

Ryan boosted himself up to try and get a make and plate. A dark colored van raced down a dirt road. He lowered himself to the ground and headed back to the house. He had some questions for Dana.

Chapter Twenty-four

Shandra and the others sat at the dining table waiting for Mrs. Alvarez to bring them coffee and dessert.

"What could be keeping her?" Alex asked, rising.

"I'll go see. You don't want to leave your other guests." Even as she said it, Shandra saw the wistfulness on both Alex and Miranda's faces to be away from Jeffrey and Genie. The two had done nothing but badger Alex about his side of the family brainwashing his grandmother to leave Genie and her mother and grandmother out of the money. It made no sense, considering Genie and her heirs weren't Porters.

Shandra hurried down the hall wondering if Ryan had arrested the housekeeper and that was why she hadn't returned after the main course had been served. Walking down the stairs to the basement, she heard voices. Before she rounded the corner, she recognized Ryan's voice.

"Where did Dana go?"

The small Hispanic woman stood in front of him her arms crossed, glaring at Ryan.

"We were wondering about dessert and coffee?" Shandra said, startling them both.

"Is that the only reason you're down here?" Ryan asked, not leaving his stance in front of the small woman.

"Yes. Dr. Porter was going to come down, but given our conversation earlier, I thought it best if I checked on her." Shandra studied the woman. She didn't appear scared, more defiant.

"This has nothing to do with our conversation. It has to do with my witnessing Dana handing things out the back door to three men who took off in a van."

Mrs. Alvarez continued to stare.

"This woman is harboring a thief." Ryan pulled out his phone. "I'm done messing around." He swiped a finger and spoke. "Hazel, send everyone at the station that can be spared over to the Narvel residence. Yes, Chief Sandberg as well. We need to search the house for a thief." He listened then said. "On second thought. I want Officer Blane to look around for a dark panel van. It has three, possibly four, men and items that were taken from the Narvel house." He closed the connection and turned to Shandra. "I'm going to stay down here and make sure no one goes out this door. Put Maxwell on the front door. When the Chief arrives, send him down to me."

She nodded and started for the stairs. "Do you want Miranda and I to search the house?"

He shook his head. "No. Wait for the Huckleberry PD. I'm going to call in some deputies too."

"Okay." She was itching to hunt through the house but instead, she followed orders. Back up in the dining room, she explained that Ryan was in the kitchen detaining the housekeeper because her daughter had been handing items out the basement door. Maxwell went to the front door and stood, his arms crossed and feet planted in a wide stance. No one would get by him.

Alex started fuming. "Dana was giving my aunt's stuff to crooks?" He stormed out of the dining room.

"Miranda, stay with him," Shandra said.

Her friend hurried out of the room.

Shandra faced Jeffrey and Genie. "We might as well go into the parlor and wait."

"Why can't we leave?" Genie asked.

"Because we were asked to stay by a lawman." Shandra waved for them to exit the dining room.

Jeffrey glanced at Maxwell standing at the outside door. "You sure you didn't have this all planned? It seems a bit suspect that you brought a mountain of a man with you to dinner when your boyfriend is chasing and accusing the staff of stealing."

She picked up on the "accusing the staff". "Is

or was Dana part of the staff in this house?"

Jeffrey walked over to the bar and poured two drinks. He handed one to Genie. "When I arrived before Christmas, Dana and her mother were the ones cleaning and putting out the Christmas decorations. I figured she was part of the staff. Then when she was caught stealing, Dana was kicked to the curb. I don't know if she found work or not. She was a nice enough kid, but I could tell she didn't like the way the old lady, Mrs. Narvel, talked to her."

Shandra filed the fact Dana had been working at the house before away. Hadn't Ryan said something about Alex thinking of her like a cousin because she had grown up in the house?

The front door rapper reverberated into the parlor.

She heard the door open.

"There you are Chief and Officer Roan." Maxwell's voice boomed through the hall and into the room.

Shandra strode out into the hall. "Ryan is downstairs, keeping an eye on the basement door."

"Thank you, Miss Higheagle." The chief's gaze went over her shoulder to the pair behind her. "Officer Roan, go relieve Detective Greer."

"The stairs are at the end of this hall," Shandra said to the officer.

He nodded and walked to the end of the hall and disappeared.

"What are you doing here?" the chief asked, remaining in the hallway.

"Maxwell and I are dinner guests of Dr. Porter and Miranda Aducci." She waved her arm into the dining room focusing on the table set for six and the half-eaten food in the dishes.

"I see." He aimed his gaze over her shoulder. "Were you also guests?"

"Yes. Jeffrey Holmes." The writer stepped out of the parlor and shook hands with the chief. "This is Genie Tapfer," he added, pulling Genie out of the room.

Her reluctance piqued Shandra's curiosity.

"Tapfer? Didn't I give you a citation for speeding the day Mrs. Narvel fell to her death?"

The woman squirmed. "I-I don't remember."

The chief pulled out his phone, hit a button, and spoke. "Hazel, Chief Sandberg. Pull up my log for the day Mrs. Narvel died."

Ryan joined them in the hall. "Chief. I caught Dana Alvarez handing stolen items out the basement door of this house to three men who got away in a van. It was too dark to make out the license."

The chief held up his finger. "Yes, that's the day. Did I give a citation to a Genevieve Tapfer on that day? Thank you, that's what I thought." The chief put his phone back in his pocket and stared at Genie.

The woman's feet shifted and her eyes wouldn't meet anyone's.

"What's this about?" Ryan asked.

"This woman doesn't remember me citing her for speeding the morning of Mrs. Narvel's death."

The chief turned his gaze to Ryan.

"Why didn't this come up when I had her in for questioning?" Ryan couldn't believe he could have had the killer locked up days ago if the citation had come up in the computer.

"It happened the day I took off to my father's funeral. I put all that information in the computer today." Chief Sandberg nodded to the woman. "You want to cuff her to keep her from going anywhere while we search for Dana?"

Ryan grasped Miss Tapfer's arm to spin her.

"Just because I don't remember getting a speeding ticket doesn't mean I killed anyone," she protested, refusing to turn.

"What time was the ticket given?" Shandra asked.

"Moments before we received the call from Mrs. Alvarez that her employer had fallen down the stairs." Chief Sandberg nodded to the cuffs.

Ryan spun the woman around and cuffed her. "You two stay right here where Maxwell can keep an eye on you." He shifted his attention to Shandra. "Where's the doc and Miranda?"

"I thought they went to the basement to talk with you and Mrs. Alvarez." Her eyes widened. "Do you think Dana did something to them?"

"Did either of you hear or see anyone go out the front door or come down the hall?" Ryan asked Shandra and Maxwell. They both shook their heads. He'd been standing in the basement watching that way out. This was an old house with few outside doors but there were windows and different roof levels for someone to escape that way.

"Chief, we need to check every room in this house. The only way out would be a window and off the roof." He reached out for Shandra's hand. "Come on, you're with me."

Ryan wasn't leaving Shandra alone. She'd go off searching on her own if he didn't bring her with him. He led her into the parlor as the chief opened closet doors.

"Why are we in here? There's no place to hide?" Shandra asked.

He pointed to the conservatory door. It would be easy for someone to hide in plain sight among all the plants. He crossed to the door and they both entered. With a finger, he motioned for her to go left and he'd go right. If Dana was hiding in here they might flush her out.

They both met back by the door.

"I don't think she's here." Shandra opened the door back into the parlor.

Chief Sandberg appeared in the parlor door. "Ready to go to the next level?"

Ryan nodded and they followed the chief up the stairs to the second floor.

Noise in the master bedroom had him motioning for Shandra to stay at the top of the stairs. He and the chief drew their weapons and approached the door. Pushing the door open, it revealed Dr. Porter and Miranda going down a list as they moved about the room.

"What are you doing?" Ryan asked, making them both jump.

"When Shandra said you caught Dana stealing, we decided to go through the inventory list and see what she'd stolen. So far we haven't found anything missing." Dr. Porter tapped the list.

"You need to go back downstairs with the others. We're conducting a search for Dana." Chief Sandberg motioned for them to leave the room.

"They weren't handing over small items," Ryan said.

Dr. Porter and Miranda left the room.

"There you two are. I thought Dana had harmed you." Shandra gave her friend a hug.

"They're going down with the others." Ryan moved to Shandra's side while waiting for the reluctant couple to descend.

"That was weird." He had never thought of Dr. Porter as materialistic and never Miranda. What were the two really doing in the old woman's room?

"What were they doing?" Shandra asked.

"Taking inventory."

Her perplexed expression matched his thoughts.

They spread out checking all the rooms and closets. They came up empty and headed to the third and the fourth floors.

Ryan couldn't believe the young woman had gotten away. He'd checked all the windows. All had screens on them. Anyone in a hurry to get away wouldn't have taken the time to replace a screen after going through the window.

"She has to be in the house somewhere." Ryan led the way down to the first floor.

Miranda stepped forward. "Can I load some of the dishes and food onto the dumb waiter and send it down to the kitchen?"

Ryan nodded to Shandra. "You can help her."

The sound of dishes being stacked and the two women's muffled voices, let him know they were keeping busy to push away the fact there could be a killer lurking in the house.

A scream sent the hair on his neck bristling.

Chapter Twenty-five

Shandra dropped the dishes she had carried to the dumb waiter and wrapped her arms around Miranda. Her friend had opened the dumbwaiter door and a hand flopped out. The arm and body attached to the hand were clothed in a familiar hoodie.

Dana Alvarez would no longer steal anything.

Ryan appeared at her side. "Shit." He shooed both she and Miranda to the far side of the room and called out, "Chief, we have a homicide!"

The room filled with people. Everyone was talking and pushing toward the hole in the wall and the body. Shandra continued to hold her friend as much to keep from falling apart as to aid Miranda.

"Why is she in there?" Miranda asked.

"I don't know. But someone in this house had to have killed her." Shandra studied Dr. Porter,

Jeffrey, and Genie. "Did Alex leave you alone at any time after you both left the dining room?"

Miranda's gaze bore into her. "What are you suggesting?"

"Nothing. Just trying to narrow down the suspects." Watching her friend's eyes narrow, Shandra had a sick feeling. Miranda could have been left alone with Dana at some time tonight. And Alex could have told her his grandmother didn't want him to marry. Miranda could have confronted Mrs. Narvel the day of her death. As quickly as the thought surfaced, she shoved it aside. The look of horror on her friend's face when she opened the dumb waiter couldn't be faked.

"Alex did go into his room to get the list while I waited in his aunt's room. But he wasn't gone long enough to kill anyone. I heard his shoes on the steps going up, a minute to get the list, and then his steps came back down." Miranda crossed her arms. "I can't believe you think he would kill his aunt and Dana."

"I've become cynical from hanging around Ryan, I guess." She listened to Ryan call in deputies and ask for the medical examiner in Warner to come.

Maxwell sidled over to them. "Looks to me like someone knocked her upside the head."

Shandra shuddered and Miranda squeaked.

"When I went to find Mrs. Alvarez, did anyone leave the dining room?" she asked the two standing near her.

Maxwell nodded. "Genie said she had to use

the powder room." He nodded toward the woman standing behind Jeffrey and avoiding looking at the body.

"How long was she gone?" Shandra had had suspicions about the woman all along.

"Five, no longer than ten minutes. Not long enough to kill her, find the dumb waiter, and put her in it." He motioned toward Genie. "I don't see any blood. That wound is really bleeding."

Chief Sandberg stood guard by the dumb waiter.

Ryan walked over to them.

Alex followed, putting his arm around Miranda, easing her away from Shandra.

Ryan met Shandra's gaze, giving her as much comfort as he could in the middle of an investigation. He shifted his attention to Miranda. "Tell me what you did when you brought the dishes over?"

Miranda glanced at the table, then at Shandra. "We stacked the plates and bowls. I put them on the tray Mrs. Alvarez left on the sideboard. I picked that up and came over here. I punched the button on the wall to bring the dumb waiter up. The door opened immediately and…" She pointed a shaky finger at the body. "Her hand fell out."

He found it interesting the body was at this floor in a room that had six people eating dinner. Dana couldn't have been in the house more than ten minutes ahead of him. The chase and retracing his steps went quickly. He'd expected her to sprint up the stairs and find a place to hide.

"How many floors does this dumbwaiter service?" he asked.

"Basement, first floor, second, and third," Dr. Porter said. "Mrs. Alvarez had the salad set when we sat down. She sent the main course up in the dumb waiter and served it. She didn't come back to take away the dishes and serve dessert. Shandra went down to see what was wrong."

Shandra added, "That's when I saw you and Mrs. Alvarez in the kitchen and you asked me to make sure no one left."

Ryan nodded. His suspicions had his stomach churning. There was only one person in the house who didn't have someone watching her the whole time.

"Chief, ask Roan to bring up Mrs. Alvarez. When they arrive, I'd like you to go down and see if there is any blood by the dumb waiter or in the kitchen."

Chief Sandberg nodded and left the room.

"You can't mean!" Miranda said loudly, her eyes wide.

"Shhh." Alex put his arms around the woman, holding her tight.

"I think it would be best if all of you go into the parlor and wait." Ryan put his arm around Shandra. "Try to keep their minds on something else if you can."

She leaned into him. "You think Mrs. Alvarez killed her own daughter?" she whispered.

He didn't have to say anything.

She sighed heavily and followed the others

across the hall.

Ryan used his time alone with the body to get a better look. From the blood drizzling into the red soaked area on the front of the hoodie, it looked like she'd been knocked alongside the head with something heavy. There were several objects in the kitchen that would do the damage he could see with his naked eye.

He heard footsteps in the hall and stepped away from the body and the hole in the wall.

Mrs. Alvarez entered first. Her gaze immediately landed on the arm hanging out of the dumb waiter. As quickly as her gaze landed, it flicked away. Her bottom lip quivered.

Ryan walked over to the table and pulled out a chair. "Mrs. Alvarez, have a seat."

She sat, her face pointed to the sideboard, but her gaze flit toward the body every few seconds as if she couldn't control her own actions.

"Why was Dana handing items out the basement door while the dinner party was going on?"

Her gaze landed on him. "I do not know what you are saying."

"Come on. You were in the kitchen preparing and serving the meal while your daughter was handing what I'm sure we'll find to be articles from this house, out the back door to three men who drove off in a van."

She stared at the sideboard again.

"I have a feeling you are not only an accessory to robbery, but you are a murderer."

Her head turned, and she stared into his eyes. "You can prove nothing. I know nothing about a robbery."

He leaned forward. "But you do know something about murder. You killed Mrs. Narvel and cool as a lifetime criminal you continued on with your work as if you hadn't a clue who could have done such a thing." Ryan pulled a chair in front of her, spun it around, and straddled the chair, folding his arms across the back and staring at the woman. "I know Mrs. Narvel told Dana you would be fired if she didn't move out. But I'm thinking you knew all about the stealing your daughter was doing. How else could she have so easily moved about the house. I think you had plans for the money you would make off the stolen goods. Mrs. Narvel didn't get around like she used to. I bet you started squirreling things away as soon as you realized she didn't go into certain rooms. And Dr. Porter, he was wrapped up in his work and research. He wouldn't notice a vase here, a picture there. And he definitely wouldn't miss jewelry. But you didn't realize Mrs. Narvel checked her jewelry every week. And when the necklace came up missing, you blamed your daughter. After all she did take it. But at your request."

The woman sniffed.

"All the items we'll pick up in the yard, that the men dropped when I chased them, will no doubt, be worth lots of money and rarely used."

Chief Sandberg entered the room at the same time sirens ended out front.

"I found something you'll want to see," the chief said. He held a towel in his hand. He unfolded the towel and revealed an iron skillet with blood and hair. "I also found an apron covered in blood, rolled up in a bloody rug, and shoved in the wine cellar."

Ryan walked over to the housekeeper as Deputy Speaks entered the room.

"Mrs. Alvarez, you are under arrest for the murder of your daughter, Dana Alvarez, and Mrs. Gladys Narvel." He waved to Speaks. "Read her her rights as you put her in the car."

This wasn't the first time he'd come across a victim murdered by a parent, however, he'd never been as disgusted as he was this time. And angry with himself. He had a notion if he'd have pressed the young woman harder the day he gave her a lift to work, she may have told him about her mother and he could have saved her life.

Chapter Twenty-six

Shandra put the last salad fork on the table and glanced out the patio doors to the smoking barbeque. Ryan was manning the grill as she finished getting everything else ready inside. It was a beautiful spring Sunday, and they'd invited Alex, Miranda, Maxwell, Ruthie and her gallery owner friends, Ted and Naomi, to a barbecue. It was the first time they'd entertained so many people at once. She was nervous and excited. The three women were her closest friends. Ryan got along fine with anyone, but he enjoyed Maxwell's company the best of the three men.

Sheba started barking. Her guests had started to arrive.

Ryan closed the lid on the grill and walked in from the patio. "Are you ready?"

"Yes. And excited. I've never had this many

people here, well excluding your family." She kissed his cheek and answered the knock at the door.

Maxwell and Ruthie walked in, carrying drinks and dessert. Behind them she caught sight of Ted and Naomi coming up the driveway.

"Come in. The drinks can go in a cooler out back. Ryan can show you. Ruthie, bring that delicious looking dessert this way." She led her friend into the kitchen.

"Every time I step in here, I wish I had this for my very own," Ruthie said.

"You have that commercial kitchen in your café."

"Yes, but this is a home cooking kitchen. This is where you pour your love into your food and serve it to the people you love." Ruthie put the dessert in the refrigerator.

Shandra studied her friend. "That is exactly how I feel when I'm in here cooking."

"You should."

There was a knock at the door and Naomi's voice. "We're here!"

"The men are in the back, we're in the kitchen!" Shandra called out.

Naomi entered, carrying French bread from the bakery. "You can't have a barbecue without Mark's bread from the Daily Donut."

"I agree. Thank you both for coming." Shandra gave them each a hug. She'd had few friends growing up and these two women had been there for her and extended their friendship to her.

Sheba barked again.

"I better go out there. Dr. Porter and Miranda might be intimidated by my cowardly dog."

The two women laughed and shooed her out of the kitchen.

To her surprise, both Miranda and Alex were scratching Sheba's belly when Shandra opened the door.

"She found two more softies, I see," Shandra said.

Miranda laughed. Her friend looked years younger and happier than she'd seen her in weeks. "I love her. She reminds me of a big, fluffy, teddy bear."

Alex took Miranda's hand, and they walked up to the door carrying a basket.

"We brought you goodies from the restaurant. Momma thought you looked skinny when she talked with you." Miranda giggled.

Shandra chuckled. "Your mother always thinks I look skinny. Come on in." She took the basket from Alex. "The guys are out on the patio. Ryan is grilling." She led Miranda into the kitchen.

Ruthie made a beeline for the younger woman. "Let me see that ring. I heard you and Dr. Porter are engaged."

Everyone oohed and ahhed over the ring.

"I was sorry to hear about Mrs. Narvel," Naomi said.

Miranda's face lost its glow. "She is a huge loss to the family and the community."

"Let's put the food on the table and join the

men outside." Shandra handed the potato salad to Miranda, the vegetable platter to Ruthie, and Naomi slid the French bread onto a platter. Shandra carried out the tossed salad.

After depositing the food, they all walked out onto the patio. The four men were in a huddle a short distance from the smoking grill.

"I thought you were watching the steaks," Shandra said, and they all jumped. The three guests made a wall between her and Ryan.

"What's going on? Did Ryan burn himself?" She tried to push through them but Maxwell only grinned and held her back.

"This is man stuff," he said and winked at Ruthie.

"Men. They can be like little boys," Ruthie replied, putting her hands on her hips.

"If the steaks are ready, the rest of the meal is." Shandra waved to the drinks sitting in ice in a chest. "Ladies, pick what you'd like to drink."

The women grabbed drinks and reentered the main room, taking places at the table. The men sauntered in, taking seats next to their women. Ryan carried in the platter of steaks and took the seat next to Shandra.

She glanced around the table and smiled at each of her guests. "It's wonderful having you all here. Enjoy the food and the company."

Everyone agreed and started dishing up. Once the food finished moving around the table, Maxwell asked, "This isn't table discussion, but we're dying to know what became of Mrs. Alvarez."

Shandra knew, with the guests she'd invited, this topic would come up. It was a relief to let everyone know what was now official.

Ryan set his fork down and met her gaze. She nodded.

"Mrs. Alvarez has been convicted on two counts of murder. She finally broke and told us she'd gone up to check on Mrs. Narvel the morning of her death. The older woman started in on her about seeing Dana sneaking around after she'd told both the girl and her mother she wasn't allowed in the house. The housekeeper knew about the previous encounter." He looked at Shandra. "The door we heard closing during the argument that Holmes taped, was Mrs. Alvarez. She'd heard her employer say she would fire her. The older woman had started noticing items missing. She, of course, accused Dana. Mrs. Alvarez grabbed her employer by the wrists, she says, trying to calm the woman. For an elderly lady, Mrs. Narvel was wiry. She slipped from the grasp and threw out the threat of firing Mrs. Alvarez as she started to go down the stairs. The housekeeper grabbed the oxygen canister by the strap. The older woman, slipped out of the strap and fell down the stairs. Mrs. Alvarez put the canister in Dr. Porter's room, in the hidden drawer, thinking no one would know to look there. Then she went down the stairs, made sure the woman was dead, and called the police."

"I would have never thought Mrs. Alvarez was so devious," Alex said.

"More than you think. Ever since your aunt

went on oxygen and was contained to the two floors and fewer rooms, your housekeeper started stealing items, hoarding them in the cellar until she could find a buyer. The night of the dinner party was the night she was getting rid of them."

"You were outside to make sure I was safe and spotted Dana handing the items over," Shandra said, putting her hand on his knee. He would always be there to protect her.

"Yes. I chased the men but they were able to get away. I was gone ten minutes at the longest. Dana had dashed into the house when I yelled at them. I knew she couldn't have run out the front without you seeing her. But I never dreamed her mother would harm her."

Everyone at the table sobered and shook their heads.

"Why did she?" Ruthie finally asked.

"Dana ran into the kitchen yelling the cops were after her and she wasn't going to be the only one going to jail. Mrs. Alvarez had been unhappy with her for some time." Ryan stopped, cleared his throat, and said, "I felt Dana wanted to tell me something when I questioned her, but I didn't ask the right questions."

Shandra put a hand on his arm and rubbed up and down. "You can't read minds. Her troubles were brought on by the mother who killed her. She is the one to blame, not you."

Ryan nodded, sipped his beer, and then continued. "As I said, Mrs. Alvarez was already angry with Dana for complaining about the stealing and not wanting to go to jail like her father. When she came in yelling, Mrs. Alvarez feared all of you in the dining room above would hear. She grabbed the pan from the stove and hit Dana on the side of the head. She didn't realize she'd killed her until she was shoving her into the dumb waiter. Then she pushed the button to send the waiter up to the first floor and ignored it."

"That's where I found poor Dana," Miranda said, quietly.

"I can't believe someone who worked for my family for all those years could hide the vileness that was underneath," Alex said.

"What about the writer and the woman claiming to be Alex's cousin?" Ruthie asked.

"They were both out to scam Mrs. Narvel. Mr. Holmes' agent was contacted about his scheme. I don't think he'll be ghost writing anymore. And Miss Tapfer…" Ryan nodded to Alex.

"Genie is my cousin twice removed from my grandmother's side of the family. Which does not make her an heir for the Porter money, unless my aunt had specifically left her something, which she did not. I told her she was welcome to visit and learn about my aunt from me, but without getting her hands on money, she doesn't seem interested." Alex shook his head. "It's sad because we really are all the family we each have."

Miranda slipped her arm around his and hugged him. "We'll start our own family."

The comment raised a smile and lit his eyes.

Shandra raised her glass. "Let's toast to good

friends and change the subject."

"Hear! Hear!" The glasses and bottles clinked and everyone started eating again. The conversation during the meal consisted of Ruthie and Maxwell telling stories about the local characters.

As everyone emptied their plates, Ruthie stood. "I'll go get the dessert."

"You don't have to, it's my party," Shandra started to stand.

"You sit, I can carry in a dessert. Maxwell, you can bring in the dessert plates." Ruthie nodded for her man to follow her.

Shandra smiled. She enjoyed watching the two and wondered when they were finally getting married. They had been a couple since she'd moved to Huckleberry.

They returned and everyone enjoyed the raspberry soufflé Ruthie served.

Once dessert was over, everyone made excuses that they needed to get going.

Shandra stood at the door, wondering why they had all left so early. She'd hoped to sit around and visit.

Ryan came up behind her. "I have wine waiting for you out back at the porch swing."

She smiled. He knew her so well. "That sounds wonderful."

They walked out onto the back patio. The birds were settling in the trees, rustling the limbs and twittering to one another.

She sat on the swing, picked up the glass of wine, and sipped, waiting for Ryan to sit beside her.

He sat, took the wine from her, and held her hand.

"Shandra, I had planned to do this up on the mountain you love, but seeing all the happy married and about to be married couples tonight, I couldn't wait."

Her heart started racing. She knew what he was about to say. Was she ready for a commitment this momentous?

"Because I know you are scared to commit, afraid I will change once that happens, I wrote up a contract and signed it. Each of the men here tonight witnessed me signing and have also signed the document as a witness. If you ever feel I am out of line, you can go to any one of them and they will straighten me out." He unfolded a piece of paper and placed it in her shaking hands.

Shandra glanced over the paper. It was a written contract saying he didn't plan to change how he treated her or how he felt about her and if he did, the three men named had his consent to help her in any way she needed.

Tears blurred her vision. "I know you would never willingly hurt me."

"Then I don't see any reason why you shouldn't say yes." He whistled. Sheba bounded out of the house and up to them. Drool hung from her lips and a red ribbon around her neck sparkled in the patio light. Shandra couldn't believe how fortunate she was to have found a man who not only knew she wanted this moment to be private, but he'd included her beloved pet.

Ryan untied the ribbon and held the most beautiful ring she'd ever seen in his fingers. "Shandra Higheagle, will you marry me?"

She leaned forward, kissed his lips, and said, "Yes. But this doesn't mean you can keep me from helping you solve murders when we get married."

About the Author

Thank you for reading *Fatal Fall*. If you enjoyed the book please leave a review. It is the best way to thank an author for an enjoyable read.

I am already plotting the next book in the series and look forward to revealing another baffling mystery for Shandra and Ryan.

Award-winning author Paty Jager and her husband raise alfalfa hay in rural eastern Oregon. On her road to publication she wrote freelance articles for two local newspapers and enjoyed her job with the County Extension service as a 4-H Program Assistant. Raising hay and cattle, riding horses, and battling rattlesnakes, she not only writes the western lifestyle, she lives it.

http://www.patyjager.net

To learn how to get FREE and discounted books sign up for Paty's free newsletter.

https://app.convertkit.com/landing_pages/93704/

Join Paty's Facebook Fan page

https://www.facebook.com/PatyJagerAuthor/

Shandra Higheagle Mystery Series

Double Duplicity
Tarnished Remains
Deadly Aim
Murderous Secrets
Killer Descent
Reservation Revenge
Yuletide Slaying
Fatal Fall

Isabella Mumphrey Adventure Series

Romantic Suspense

Secrets of a Mayan Moon
Secrets of an Aztec Temple
Secrets of a Hopi Blue Star

Thank you for purchasing this Windtree Press
publication. For other books of the heart, please visit
our website at www.windtreepress.com.

For questions or more information contact us
at info@windtreepress.com.

Windtree Press
www.windtreepress.com

Hillsboro, OR

www.ingramcontent.com/pod-product-compliance
Lightning Source LLC
Chambersburg PA
CBHW070921190726
48292CB00004B/1058